SORRY!...
How Many Times?

CHRISTINE DIGGINS

The characters and events portrayed in this book are fictitious. Any similarity to real persons, living or dead, is coincidental and not intended by the author.

No part of this book may be reproduced, or stored in a retrieval system, or transmitted in any form or by any means, electronic, mechanical, photocopying, recording, or otherwise, without express written permission of the publisher.

Copyright © 2023 Christine Diggins
All rights reserved

CHAPTER 1

It was late summer 1965. The streets of Manchester were quiet. The time of year when the nights were drawing in early and the weather; although not unpleasant, had a distinctive chill in the evening air. Raining for the past two days, the sort of days which made you want to curl up in front of a lovely glowing red fire, cosily ensconced indoors.

Feeling very lazy and relaxed, the television had the ten-o'clock news on in the corner of the room. Her three-month-old baby was fed, changed, and sleeping contentedly in Jenny's arms. She leaned back against the cushioned arm of the sofa and lifted her feet gently up off the floor. Soon she would go to her bed but for now she stretched out comfortably staring up at the yellowing ceiling, her thoughts wandered into another way of life, one that she would never have but could dream about. The baby's soft breathing rhythm lulled

Jenny and gradually she drifted off into a comforting sleep.

Suddenly her eyes sprang open. Could that have been the front door opening? Jenny remembered she had forgotten to lock it. She listened intently, every nerve in her body was alert to the slightest sound. A faint rattle of the room door handle made her sit up abruptly, the baby still in her arms fast asleep. The room became quiet again, then almost as if she had willed it, the familiar rattle came again.

Quickly rising from the sofa, she laid the sleeping baby down and moved to get a better view of the room door. Every nerve in her body taught, her feet rooted to the spot as her eyes scanned the brass doorknob for the slightest of movement. After what appeared to be an age, Jenny began to relax a little telling herself that she had been mistaken. In her dreamy state, could it have been possible she had dreamt hearing the noise? Glancing down towards the sleeping child, her tension eased, she managed a smile, thinking herself a little foolish. It was about time mum and daughter got off to bed she thought. In the morning, her husband would be home and they would have a good laugh at her foolishness.

Moving round to the front of the hearth, Jenny proceeded to attend to the fire in preparation for retiring to bed. Instinctively, her body tensed and she once again became rigid. No! it was not a mistake, there was the noise again! This time was more definite than the last. Swinging around with determined courage and without further thought, she called out, "Who's there? Is anybody there?"

Instantly the doorknob ceased moving as though someone had let it go suddenly. Jenny became tense again, her eyes transfixed on that brass knob. With her hands tightly clenched, she somehow found the courage to call out again, "Roy...Oh Roy answer me, is that you?" There was no reply, only the deafening silence that seemed to engulf the mind when afraid. Jenny watched and waited and then it happened again, the knob was being turned slowly round and round, "Please, who is it? If it's you Roy, stop fooling around and come in! You're scaring me!"

The knob stopped turning again as though the hand that had been on it was snatched away. The fear became too much for Jenny and she suddenly leapt into action. Rushing around the sofa and scooping up the fair-haired sleeping baby she fled towards the kitchen.

On reaching the back door she took a towel down from the hook and wrapped it as fast as she could over the child's head with one hand while the other hand grasped the door handle and flung the door wide open. Rushing out, the cold night air caught at her breath, but without pausing she ran across the yard as if the devil himself was after her.

Banging on the first door across the yard, no-one answered and without hesitating any longer she ran to the next and thumped as hard as she could until she heard someone undoing the bolt and the lock. Not waiting to be invited in or yet giving any explanation, Jenny fled inside to safety.

"What the devil!" The woman holding open the door was knocked aside with the speed of Jenny's entrance. "Have you no manners? Usually, a person waits to be asked to come in first." It was clear that this woman was taken aback by the forced entry of this person but noticing the baby she forgot her indignation and immediately became concerned. "What's wrong, is the baby all right?" Without waiting for a reply, she quickly shut the door and went to look at the sleeping child cradled in Jenny's arms.

For a moment Jenny couldn't speak, fear was

gripping every part of her body. The dryness of her mouth was making it difficult to form any words. Eventually, she managed to find her voice, "Please, oh please help me! There's someone in my house, a burglar, a madman even," Jenny was now almost hysterical and shaking from head to foot.

"Here, give the baby to me and calm down a bit, you're safe now." The woman gently lifted the baby from Jenny's trembling arms and steered her into the warmth of the living room. "Sit yourself down and tell me what's happened."

Jenny resisted a little then began, "You don't understand, there really is someone in there and it's not Roy my husband. I called out his name and he didn't answer, so how could it be him?" Tears overcame her and, feeling her legs had turned to jelly, she sank down into the armchair putting her head in her hands, she continued between sobs, "I know I got frightened, and I should have seen who it was, but it wasn't Roy as he is working and besides, he wouldn't frighten me like that."

"There, there, come on now. Don't take on so." The woman patted the top of Jenny's head. "If you say there's someone in your house, then we shall have to deal with it. Though, I have no man of my own in the house right now, he's at work you see, on nights this week."

The woman laid the baby gently down onto her sofa and covered the little girl with the towel. "Your baby will be alright there for now. Will you be alright if I nip next door and get Stan to sort this?" Without waiting for a reply, the woman quickly went out the front door and banged on the next door of the terraced houses.

Jenny could hear muffled voices, which gradually got clearer as two people entered the front door of the house. A tall thin man stood within the door frame, "Now then young lass, what's all this I'm hearing?" He sounded stern, but there was also a note of kindly concern in his voice. Without any hesitation Jenny told him of her ordeal and flight across the yard. "Well now, if what you tell me is true, I shall have to get the police." The man spoke in a calm manner trying to reassure Jenny he had things under control.

"Oh no, must you involve the police? Couldn't you just go across to my house yourself and see for sure if anyone is there?" Jenny pleaded.

"And get my head bashed in for my trouble! No; I don't think so, best to get the police then if there is someone there, they can handle it better than me." Without waiting for Jenny to speak again, he went off to telephone the police from the phone box on the corner of the street.

Half an hour later, Jenny was back in her own home, cradling her daughter in her arms and feeling much calmer, but extremely confused. She was surrounded by three burley policemen and was standing open mouthed in amazement at the man sitting in the tatty old armchair. Her eyes were not deceiving her, though she was finding great difficulty in taking in the scene.

The tallest policeman; one who looked important, now spoke in a deep, but gentle voice, "You say this here is your husband, Roy, and that he didn't answer when you called out his name before?" Jenny could only nod her head as she stared in disbelief at her husband whose face was expressionless as he glared up at her.

"Well now," the policeman spoke again." this is a strange situation we have here." He now turned to the young man in the armchair and leaned menacingly over him and with a wagging finger, an inch from the pale blue staring eyes, he spoke in an angry manner, "Are you aware of the trouble you've caused here tonight?" He did not wait for any reply but continued, "this young wife of yours has been scared out of her wits by your foolishness. Playing practical jokes is one thing, but to knowingly make her fear for her life is another matter. Just what did you expect her reaction would be? Obviously, she would run to safety for herself and the child. You disgust me!" He was clearly very annoyed with Roy.

He now moved menacingly closer. His face not six inches from Roy, "I have your face stored in here," he tapped his forehead, "and if you step out of line again, I'll have you arrested and make no mistake." With that he stood up and stepped back, turning towards Jenny as he did so. Telling her not to be afraid anymore and asked if she wanted any charges to be brought against her husband. Jenny shook her head and explained that Roy may be foolish, but he was not a bad person, and she was just glad it was all sorted out.

Thanking the policemen one by one as they left the house she closed and locked the door behind them. Jenny reflected on her words to the policeman, "not a bad person", huh, how she wished that were true.

He may be all right most of the time, but when he had been out drinking with his mates, that was another matter. What puzzled Jenny the most was why was he even out drinking when he should have been at work on night shift.

Without even speaking to her husband, she left the room with the baby still sleeping in her arms and disappeared up to bed where she turned the key in the lock without any thought for him or where he would sleep that night. Her anger was almost too much to bear but apart from a few tears she was determined not to give in to her feelings.

CHAPTER 2

When Jenny came downstairs the next morning, Roy was nowhere to be seen. Likely he had gone to work early to avoid facing her. Jenny now believed he had not had to work the night shift and that had just been an excuse to go out with his mates. He had slept on the sofa, leaving her to spend the night alone in the bedroom. It had been a restless night for Jenny, and she felt tired and not quite herself. The night before had continued to be at the forefront of her mind. She felt so many emotions, but most of all anger at Roy for putting her through that.

Baby Amy let out a loud cry bringing Jenny out of her thoughts. She picked up the little girl and prepared to give her the morning feed. After dressing Amy, she would go to the baby clinic and afterwards visit her mum for the rest of the morning. Her mum was a very calm woman, nothing appeared to bother her, and

Jenny knew that an hour in her company would help her to feel less upset by the previous night's happenings.

Just as Jenny finished dressing Amy and laying her down in the pram, there was a knocking on the back door. Jenny knew no-one usually came to the back door so assumed it might be the woman who had helped her. On opening the door Jenny's guess was correct for there stood the woman from the night before.

"Hello, I'm Mary from across the yard. I was wondering how you are after all the goings on last night, so decided to pop over and check on you. One of the policemen came to tell me who it was and the problem was resolved. I couldn't quite get my head around that it was your husband who had frightened you like that."

"Oh, please come in. I am all right just a bit shaken up but mostly I feel angry at my husband," Jenny felt pleased though that the woman cared enough to come and check on her. "You already know the intruder turned out to be my husband Roy who thought it was a good idea to play a joke on me. Would you like a cup of tea? I have just put Amy down for her morning nap and was just about to make some tea." Jenny lied.

"Well, I don't want to take up too much of your time, I know you must be busy, but tea would be nice and a chat if you have time. What a todo your husband frightening you like that. I hope you told him off."

"I was too upset to even speak to him but the policeman gave him a right telling off and a warning. Pleased, sit yourself down and I'll only be a minute making the tea." Jenny went to the kitchen then called out as an afterthought, "Would you like a biscuit with your tea?"

"No thanks, just the tea will be fine. I hope it's no trouble, but I could hardly sleep worrying that you and the baby were alright. I realised though that the police must have dealt with it when one of them came to thank me for my help."

When Jenny came back into the room, Mary was by the pram quietly looking down at the sleeping baby. On seeing Jenny entering, two cups of tea in hand, she moved to sit down on the armchair. Jenny placed the cups of tea on the coffee table and sat in the other chair, opposite her. The night before when Jenny had been in such a state, she hadn't taken a lot of notice of what the woman looked like. Now she could see that the woman was probably younger than she had thought last night, perhaps only a few years older than herself.

"Your baby is beautiful, how old is she?" The woman interrupted Jenny's thoughts.

"My daughter is three months old, and we called her Amy after her great granny who sadly is no longer alive so will never meet my Amy." Jenny sipped the refreshing tea and then continued, "Roy and I have only been married for eighteen months and we hadn't planned on having children yet, but Amy surprised us. I fell pregnant after only a few months of our marriage."

The woman gave a nervous laugh saying, "These things have a habit of happening when you least expect them, but a baby is such a precious thing to have. You are so lucky."

"Do you have any children? Jenny had not had time to get to know her neighbours and although sounding nosey she felt it was right to ask this seeing as the woman had asked about Amy.

Mary looked down at the floor and Jenny thought she was not going to answer her. Then as she looked up again, she spoke rather hesitantly. "No, we haven't been blessed with a child. At least not yet and I am ever hopeful it will happen, but I am twenty-six and John, my husband is thirty, so we are getting older all the time. She paused to drink some tea, "By the way I don't know your name." She sounded as if she were trying to be cheerful whilst changing the subject and Jenny guessed she really would love to have a child of her own.

"I'm Jenny…Jenny Crabtree and I'm twenty-two years old. I'm sorry you haven't had a baby yet, but my mum was thirty-two when she had me so don't think it won't happen, there is plenty of time. You're still young."

Mary said that Jenny was probably correct, and she still had time and then she stood up saying she must be going but hoped that they might be friends and she could visit again. To which Jenny replied that it was good of her to come over and that she would be very happy to be friends stating that maybe next time she could pay her a visit. With one more look at Amy in her pram Mary left by the back door.

After Mary left Jenny got ready to go to the baby clinic with Amy. It was possibly time for Amy to have a vaccination and Jenny was apprehensive about this. She needn't have worried; all went well, and Jenny chastised herself for being anxious. Amy was doing well, had put weight on and was feeding ok so Jenny was pleased with the outcome of the visit.

They had been at her parent's home for half an hour and Betty, her mum, was giving Amy her bottle feed. She loved it when Jenny brought Amy to visit. It was her first grandchild and so she doted on her. Betty's attention was all on the baby, but she had noticed that Jenny was very quiet when usually she was quite a chatterbox and was always ready to tell her mum everything that had happened since her last visit.

With feeding over and baby Amy now sleeping, Betty turned her attention onto Jenny. "Are you ok Jenny, you're very quiet today?" They were now having their morning coffee, "Is Roy getting on all right? Don't tell me you and he have been arguing again. What has he got a problem with this time? Betty was not giving Jenny time to answer before she continued, "I told you didn't I that you were marrying too soon and should have waited another year! He is never satisfied, got a loving wife and a gorgeous daughter, there's no pleasing him."

Jenny quickly spoke before her mum could say anymore, "Aww mum don't go on about him that way. Roy and me haven't been arguing and our marriage is working just fine." Jenny lied and had decided not to tell her mum about the night before and the stupid joke Roy had played on her, knowing that she would never hear the last of it from mum and dad if she had informed Betty of it.

"Well, something is the matter, I can see you're down and not your usual cheerful self today."

"It's nothing really, going to the baby clinic made me anxious. Everything went well so I am ok now. I didn't sleep well and woke up with a headache, so I am feeling a bit down, but I will be all right again soon." Jenny also decided not to mention Mary's visit because it would lead to explaining why she had done so.

The rest of the morning they chatted about this and that and her mum stayed clear of the subject of Jenny's marriage. She wasn't too keen on Roy; thought he was a bit all for himself and did not prioritise his responsibilities when it came to helping Jenny care for

Amy. One thing she did remember to mention was that Jenny's brother Tom was coming home on leave and she wanted them all to have a family dinner this coming Sunday, so would Jenny and Roy be sure to come?

Tom was Jenny's older brother, who had joined the army two years ago. She knew he would be going overseas soon so promised her mum that they would be sure to come to Sunday dinner. Although Jenny knew she would have her work cut out getting Roy to agree to come. He knew that her mum and dad had not been altogether pleased at her marriage to him, but they couldn't prevent it because Jenny was old enough to make her own decisions.

It was soon mid-day and Jenny left her mum with the understanding she would see her on Sunday. Jenny called at the shop on her way back home and was going to try to get a nap in the afternoon so she could be on top form to tackle Roy when he came home from work.

CHAPTER 3

A week later, the atmosphere in the house was still somewhat tense. Jenny was barely speaking to Roy but not just because of the conversation she had with him over the frightening episode, it was also because he refused to come with her to the Sunday lunch which she had promised her mum they would attend.

When she questioned Roy about why he did what he did on the night of frightening her, he wasn't very apologetic but accused her of not having a sense of humour as he had thought it would be funny to play a trick on her. He was also not pleased with her for calling in the police and said that was a bit over the top. No amount of arguing with him could make him see her point of view and in the end, she gave up trying.

Going to the family lunch by herself with Amy

made for some awkward conversations with her mum and dad as to why Roy was absent. Not entirely sure they believed her when she told them he wasn't very well with stomach pains and had thought it would be best not to eat anything but to rest up for the day. From what Betty had to say made it sound like she did not believe a word of it.

Tom, Jenny's brother came to her rescue by interrupting the conversation and asking about Amy. "She is growing so fast and has a beautiful smile," he said whilst playfully tickling her tummy. "How did you ever manage to get such a pretty baby with a face like yours?" He teased.

She gave his arm a shove and cheekily answered, "Well it must run in the family then, but your face is far uglier than mine" Jenny ducked just in time to avoid the slap Tom playfully aimed at her. Her brother had always teased her from as long as she could remember. "You can pick her up if you like. She doesn't bite, well has never done before. Anyway, if she doesn't like you then she just might make you her first victim. He eagerly picked up Amy and sat down in the armchair so he could put her on his knee. He appeared to be a natural with a baby for Amy did not take her eyes off him whilst he gently spoke to her.

The lunch and visit went reasonably well, and no-one mentioned Roy again until Jenny was leaving to go home. At the door, her dad put a gentle arm around her and bending closer, told her that if ever she needed to come home if marriage got too much, then he would welcome her with open arms and saying that there would always be a home there for her.

The following week was not much better than the last. Although, on speaking terms, Jenny only made conversation with Roy when it was necessary. Roy on the other hand made extra effort to be what he thought was being a good husband. He helped to feed Amy and kept her occupied while Jenny was busy. Then surprised Jenny by offering to make lunch on the Sunday whilst she put her feet up and read a magazine. Jenny wasn't fooled by any of this because Roy had done the same on several occasions after they had quarrelled, but never ever saying he was sorry was something Jenny had learned to accept.

It was four weeks later, after one of Jenny's many visits to her mum that she was faced with quite a shock. What Roy told her that evening would bring a change to their lives. After Amy had been fed and put to bed, Roy suggested that Jenny should sit down because he had something important to tell her.

After making herself comfortable on the sofa he then told her he had been dismissed from his job immediately after fighting with another worker and damaging property. Not expecting to hear this, Jenny sat speechless. She could hardly take in his words and asked him to repeat what he had just said. After what seemed like ages, she managed to find her voice.

"What are we going to do now? There won't be any money coming in. Amy needs food and clothes; she is growing so fast I can hardly keep up with new things for her." Jenny could feel a lump rising in her throat, but she wasn't going to cry, telling herself that wouldn't solve anything. Roy hadn't spoken again but now seeing his wife upset he tried to reassure her.

"Don't worry about anything because tomorrow I will sign on the dole. That will give us money till I can find another job." It all sounded so easy to repair the damage losing his job had done, "Tomorrow I will start to look for another job and I won't stop till I get one." Roy sounded pleased and appeared to have forgotten the reasons why he got the sack, but Jenny was quick to remind him.

"Oh, you…you think it will be so easy to walk right into another job when you were dismissed for fighting. That doesn't sound too good to me let alone an employer. Who is going to take a chance on employing a violent man?" Now Jenny did burst into tears, and she rocked back and forth with her head in her hands.

"Please Jenny, don't be like this, don't be so negative. I feel really bad about what has happened, but I promise to do my best to put it right." He appeared remorseful but Jenny didn't feel there could be any hope for him to change the situation. At least not as quickly as he thought he could.

She could not face him anymore; anger was rising in her, but she didn't want to have another argument so without looking at him she left the room and went upstairs to bed. On her own in the bedroom, she let the tears flow and the sobbing showed how upset she was at this news. As the sobbing got less and less, she dried her eyes and lay there on the bed quietly staring up at the ceiling. She was thinking about just how young she was and not equipped to deal with what she saw as big problems.

Believing that Roy would find it difficult to get

another job, all she could see was that they were going to struggle, maybe even not able to pay the rent and become homeless. She even thought about asking her parents for help. Maybe they could go and live with them for a while, but no they wouldn't get on with Roy, so she dismissed that solution. Eventually she calmed down enough to try to think about solutions to the problem but finally she could not decide on anything and could only hope that Roy would sort things out. With that thought in her mind she rolled onto her side and drifted off to sleep.

After four weeks of trying to find employment, Roy was becoming desperate and running out of ideas. Jenny tried to help by scouring the ads in the newspaper, but every job advert came to nothing. After informing her parents of their situation, even her dad had asked around to see if he could find Roy a job. Her dad had given Jenny some money saying it was to tide her over until Roy was working again. Jenny tried to refuse the money, but her dad was having none of it and in the end, Jenny accepted saying it was only a loan and she would pay him back. Secretly she was thankful for the money knowing the rent was due and she had been worried because there was no money to pay it. Now she could stop worrying, the rent could be paid.

It was Jenny's brother Tom who while visiting his parents for the weekend before going off to an army camp in Germany, came up with an idea which might be a solution to Roy's predicament. He had asked Roy to join him at the pub for a chat and a beer. Jenny was suspicious at what her brother might be up to. Tom had not taken Roy out for a drink before but Roy, although also puzzled, had agreed to go.

It was a Saturday afternoon when Roy went to the pub with Tom. Jenny was visiting her parents with Amy and although she questioned them about the reason for this sudden invitation by Roy, they didn't know or wouldn't say so she could only wait until Roy and Tom came back home. The waiting was agonising for Jenny and her mum could see it was stressing her daughter not to know. She really didn't know why Tom had suddenly wanted to see Roy. They were in the dark as much as Jenny was.

It was mid-afternoon when the two men returned home. Roy was being very secretive about their visit to the pub, just telling Jenny he may have news of employment, but she would have to wait until they went home before he told her. For once Jenny's parents were being polite to Roy suggesting that he and their daughter should stay for tea. Roy looked towards Jenny then smiling, he accepted the offer, so Jenny would have a bit longer to wait but did not want to upset her parents by turning them down.

Roy was silent on the journey home and Jenny decided it was better to wait until she had sorted Amy out. After the baby was asleep, they would be able to talk so she didn't speak much to Roy only saying how nice it had been to have a family tea together at last. When at last she and Roy could have a conversation alone together, Jenny once more was shocked at what Roy had to say about his visit to the pub with Tom. Never could she have imagined what they had talked about, but remembering that Roy had told her earlier it was about employment for him she could not believe Roy was considering what Tom had suggested.

He told Jenny he was going to sign up to join the army. Tom had put the idea to him and had described what sort of life he and Jenny could expect. Roy did not need much time to think about it, but had told Tom that he wanted to join up as soon as he was able to and got all the information on how to do this from Tom.

"Believe me Jenny when I tell you that this will be

the best for both of us. I will earn a wage and we will be given a place to live together so you and Amy will be safe and you free from worrying about the lack of money."

Jenny could only stare at Roy in disbelief. It took her a while to let all this sink in and then when she could speak, she was full of questions. "Have you really thought about what life as a soldier would be like? I would have to leave my parents to live who knows where, maybe even in another country. I am not sure if I can do that and take Amy away from them, so they won't see her growing up."

"Don't you think I know all that? You could come home often with Amy to visit, and Tom has given me some idea about training and all that the army has to offer. I really want to do this Jenny, please be on my side. It is a way for me to provide for us."

"You seem to have made up your mind, but how do you know they will let you join? Jenny is still full of doubts. "Will they be willing to accept you when they know the reason you were sacked from your previous job?"

"You're right, I don't know if they will take me,

but I won't know unless I try. Tom is so sure I won't have any trouble joining up as he says there is a lot of discipline in the army and I will learn to control my anger by channelling it into fighting for a reason. The pay is good as a bonus so what do I have to lose by trying to join? I can't do this without you being with me on this though."

Listening to Roy, she had not seen him so enthusiastic about anything before and she was slowly beginning to think it may be one way to solve their problems, but only if Roy was really serious about it. Could she get as excited about this as Roy appeared to be? No, she needed more time to process her thoughts on this, but she would not stand in her husband's way and would support his decision for him to try and get into the army.

CHAPTER 4

Jenny really hadn't been convinced that her husband would be able to join the army. But now here she was packing his clothes in preparation for him going to an army camp to begin his training. Roy came home very excited at having been accepted for the British Army and was to report to the Barracks in a week's time. He would be going there alone and Jenny would join him just as soon as army quarters were provided, such as a house or flat for her and Roy to live in.

Mary had popped in for a chat and only just left again. They had become good friends, visiting each other daily. She was always ready to listen to Jenny getting her woes off her chest and of course loved playing with Amy or just looking at her if she happened to be asleep. Today, Mary had some good news that she and John had been accepted for a new family planning treatment and hopeful that if it worked, she would become pregnant. Jenny did not have the heart to tell her about Roy going into the army, she knew Mary would miss her. Mary didn't have any other friends and especially if she did get pregnant that would be an exciting time and Jenny knew she might not be around to share that with her. So, Jenny had decided that her news could wait and anyway it might be months before she had to leave and join Roy.

Jenny's mum and dad were pleased about Roy having joined the army. Tom had told them what he had been discussing with Roy at the pub. So, when Jenny told them that Roy had been accepted and when he would be leaving, her parents wanted to know if she would be happy moving away from them. Trying not to sound too pleased she told them she was happy Roy had joined up, but was a bit anxious about leaving the only place she had called home and of course leaving them. Betty told Jenny not to worry about them and although they would miss her and Amy, they would visit whenever they were able, even if that was another country. So that left only one thing to be anxious about and that was whether she would like being a soldier's wife. She let out a big sigh and decided in her mind that she would make a go of it whatever it was like.

On the day Roy was leaving to start his journey in the army, Jenny was full of mixed emotions. Happy she would not have any more money worries; sad Roy was leaving and anxious for what the future held for them. Roy had been happy the past few weeks and there had been no more arguments. He had even taken Jenny out for a meal at the Chinese Restaurant two nights previously and after a few glasses of wine, Jenny became a little tipsy and the evening was rounded off with a night of passion. Mary had looked after Amy and because Jenny had by now told her what the future held for her and Amy, Mary told Jenny she was happy to spend as much time as possible with Amy before it would be their turn to leave.

***

Two months had passed which had gone by so slowly for Jenny. She had found it lonely being on her own especially in the evenings after Amy had gone to bed. Mary had taken Amy out in her pram for a walk on most days whenever the weather permitted and when John was working nights, had come to Jenny's house and spent the evening with her. Jenny had already packed some of her things in anticipation of joining Roy and for something to occupy her time. He had written to her every week and updated her in his letters of his training progress. Writing that he found it quite hard, but had made some friends to go out with at weekends, mostly to the pub and had learned a lot about being a soldier.

Jenny was a bit upset that he hadn't once mentioned he was missing her or Amy, but he did write that they were on the list for accommodation and the officer in charge of these things had assured him it would only be a short time away and Jenny could be joining him there. The officer couldn't have told Roy the truth because it was another two months and still no news of a date to join him, however, Roy had written that it was to be his passing out parade and wanted Jenny to be there to see it.

The day of Roy's passing out parade came and would mean he would be serving as a soldier in an Infantry regiment for the Queen and country. After this day Roy would be assigned duties to carry out and would sometimes have to go away on operations with exercises of how to fight the enemy. Roy told Jenny that afterwards he would be a real fighting soldier.

Jenny wasn't sure which he was most excited about, becoming a soldier or the fighting side of this. Nevertheless, she was happy for him and had to admit felt a sense of pride that her husband had succeeded in getting through the training for the time he had been there without getting into any trouble.

Accompanied by her parents while leaving Amy at home in the care of Mary who was so happy to be having Amy to herself. At the army camp Jenny and her parents had found a good spot on the parade ground with other family members who were there to watch their sons and brothers. Roy being an only child, Mrs Crabtree would have been the only other one to come today as his father had died of a heart attack six years ago, but she could not get the time off from her job.

Fifteen minutes later, the army band began playing and there was a mass of marching soldiers coming onto the parade ground. It was a wonderful site to see them marching in unison and positioning themselves into groups. It had been fascinating seeing the passing out parade, Jenny had told Roy's Commanding Officer who had been making his way around the families and had arrived at her side. He told

Jenny he was pleased to meet her and hoped she was enjoying the day. The best part of their brief chat was when he had praised Roy and said he had the makings of a fine soldier.

Afterwards Jenny and her parents had only just found a seat when Roy came to join them. There were two other soldiers with him who he introduced as Pete and Dave, telling Jenny they didn't have any family members there today, so he had invited them to join them. Roy suggested they should get some food from the buffet and the two lads told him to stay with Jenny and they would get the food.

The next hour was full of chatter and Jenny even had a glass of champagne. Two of the other army wives came up to Jenny for a chat and they told her that when they were all finally living at the camp, they could all meet up at the park with their youngsters, perhaps on one afternoon assuming the weather would be fine. Jenny accepted the invitation and agreed to be there. They went away suggesting that their husbands could swap details of addresses when they all had accommodations and were finally living in the camp.

Roy was pleased that his wife would have friends soon after arriving at the camp. She also liked his two friends and chatted easily with them. She found out that Pete wasn't married and his mum was in a nursing home, and he had no other relatives, but that Dave was married and separated from his wife and had two young sons, but didn't see them very often. Jenny felt sorry that they had no family come to see the parade and she told them they could come round anytime for a cuppa when she eventually was living there, which they both agreed would be great and thanked her for the invite.

Four weeks after the parade day, Roy finally had news of accommodation at the camp for them to be together. A house awaited her and Amy's arrival, with her parents taking them to join her husband. Her dad had borrowed a small works van to transport all the belongings Jenny wanted to take with her. No furniture would need to go with her because the house was furnished with army belongings. Everything would be provided including pots, pans, cutlery, bedding and even a cot for Amy. So, Jenny and Roy's small number of furnishings were to be stored in the spare bedroom at her parent's home until they might need them again. Jenny had been astounded that everything a home required would be provided for them and it did cross her mind how she might find not having her own things around would suit her. So had decided to take some possessions with her from her current home and make the new army place more homely.

The day of leaving for a new life as an army wife with the adventures it would bring had arrived. Mary was having one last hold of Amy and there were tears, but Jenny had promised to come back for a visit soon reminding Mary that she would need her fill of gossip and news. Jenny and her dad were busy putting boxes and suitcases into the van. It was difficult to fit everything in around Amy's pram which had to go with them to the camp. Betty had suggested leaving the pram behind at their home and she would give Jenny money to buy a pushchair which could be more suitable for Amy as she was now one year old. Jenny wouldn't hear of any such thing. Although Amy was a year old, Jenny felt she was better in her pram for now.

This proved to be a wrong decision because after arriving at the camp and although the house was very nice, it was at the top of a steep hill and the shops that Jenny would have to visit were at the bottom end of the hill. They were soon to find this out when, shortly after arriving, it was decided that some groceries were required. Jenny and Betty set off down the hill to the shops with Amy in her pram while the men unpacked the belongings from the van.

They found there was an adequate number of shops to buy things from, so all went well until the return journey home and having to push the pram up the hill back to the house had required both women to push the pram. When they finally got back to the house, they were both exhausted and after telling Jenny's dad about their ordeal, he placed some money on the table and refused to accept a no from Jenny to buy a pushchair for Amy. She didn't have a choice when her dad quickly loaded the pram back into the van to take back home with them.

Later that week Roy decided it would be good to give Jenny a tour around the camp so she would get the feel of the place. After placing Amy in her new pushchair, they set off, firstly towards the entrance to the main barracks. Here Jenny saw there were soldiers on guard duty so that not just anyone could enter. They passed the parade ground where she had seen Roy's passing out parade then walked past a large building with many windows and Roy told Jenny his room had been in there for the past few months while he waited for her to join him.

After leaving the barracks, Roy took them a different way home and they stopped at a park. He mentioned that this would be the park she would be meeting her new friends at. They pushed Amy for a while on a swing then sat on a bench and Roy asked her what she thought of the place and was she happy being there with him. Her reply was that she liked what she had seen so far but as for being happy there, that would be something he should ask her later when she would have had time to settle in.

CHAPTER 5

It had been three weeks since that day and the weeks had gone by in a whirr of unpacking their small possessions, getting used to shopping and finding her way around. Jenny then had to register and visit the baby clinic so Amy could continue her vaccination and health check programme. After Roy brought home the addresses of the two friends she met at the parade, she went round to visit each one and later they visited her. During one of these visits, Carol, one of the friends, had suggested although it was November they should meet at the park on the following Tuesday. So, Jenny had agreed to be there at two and Carol promised to let Andrea the other friend know and hoped she would agree to join them. Andrea had wanted to join in and promised to see them both at the park.

On the first visit to the park, they chatted mostly about their children. Carol had two, the oldest a boy was nearly three and the youngest, a girl, had just had her first birthday, so Amy was just a little older. Andrea had only a two-year-old girl who appeared to be very demanding and hard work for her mum. The meet up was very enjoyable for Jenny, and she felt so pleased that she had two friends whom she got on with. Even so it had been difficult for Jenny not to be able to visit her mum every week, but she was determined to settle down and accept she was now an army wife with all that entailed. Besides, it would be Christmas soon and her parents had agreed it would be better for them to come and spend two days with Jenny and Roy at the army camp especially as Amy would be having her first proper Christmas with presents and decorations.

Thinking of decorations reminded Jenny that she would have to speak to Roy about going shopping soon for presents and decorations as well as planning what food they will need for the Two days over Christmas. Roy wasn't too keen on doing this when Jenny brought it up in a conversation but after a bit of an argument, he agreed to go on the Saturday of the first week in December. He had kept to his agreement and now there was two more weeks before her parents would be arriving for the festivities. Jenny was excited to be seeing them again but mainly to see Amy's face on

Christmas morning when she opened all her presents. Now she had started walking, playtime with her mum or dad had become more interesting. Another reason for Jenny's excitement was that there was a dinner and dance in the evening of Saturday, one week before Christmas day.

When the day of the dance arrived. Jenny wore a pink dress with a cream lace overlay on the bodice and cream strappy shoes. She felt so grown up having never been to such a special dance they were on their way to. Roy looked very handsome in his light grey suit with blue shirt and navy-blue tie. Very different from his usual jeans and tee shirt. Jenny had made sure Amy was safely asleep in her bed when they left her in the care of Dave. He had not wanted to go to the dance saying it would mainly be couples who were there and anyway, he had experience with children having two of his own and it would be a break from the barrack accommodation to look after Amy for them.

At the barracks, Jenny saw Carol and her husband seated at one of the tables. The tables were all for six and placed on one side of the room with the other side left for dancing. Roy had no objection to joining them at the table saying that Kevin was in the same regiment, so they were mates. Another of Roy's mates also joined them with his wife who was introduced to Jenny as Beryl.

The evening was great with lots of good food from the buffet and a great band playing up to date music. Jenny was hardly off the dance floor as one soldier after another asked her to dance with them.

As for Roy he was on his best behaviour, dancing with some of the other blokes' wives. He saved the last waltz for Jenny and as they smooched their way around the dance floor to the tone of 'Save the last dance for me' Jenny, being a little tipsy, nuzzled her husband's neck and whispered to him in his ear that she loved him very much.

It all ended too soon and after many goodbyes, kisses and cries of Merry Christmas everyone made their way home. Roy thanked Dave for looking after Amy whom he told them had not woken at all. Roy promised him a couple of drinks next time they went to the pub and finally it was after midnight when they made their way up to bed and slept soundly after a very passionate session of lovemaking.

It was three days before Christmas Eve and Jenny

had spent the afternoon decorating the house with streamers, tinsel, and balloons. She had met up with Carol at Andrea's home for morning coffee and cake and exchanged gifts for each of the children. The women had bought each other chocolates so everyone was in a happy mood chatting about the coming festivities. It had been a very pleasant morning and now Jenny was enjoying putting up Christmas decorations which Roy had adamantly refused to get involved with. Amy was having her afternoon nap which gave Jenny some time to herself. Roy had promised to help with decorating the tree in the evening, so all was going well with the preparations.

That evening, Roy said he was too tired to do the tree and agreed to help Jenny the following evening. Jenny also felt drained from the day's work and so Roy did not get any objections from her. She did remind him that there was very little time to put the tree up, so it must go up the next day. After Amy had been tucked up in bed, Jenny felt quite tired and was also looking forward to an early night, but then Roy announced that he had promised some of his mates he would join them at the pub for a drink before Christmas. Jenny wasn't pleased and she had decided that this was the reason he had put off doing the tree until tomorrow. Sounding cross, she told him to go but not to be too late home because he had to be up early to be at the barracks for eight. He promised he would only stay for an hour and wouldn't drink much beer. After he left, Jenny lay cuddled in a blanket on the sofa with her feet up. She tried to read her book, but soon drifted off to sleep.

***

Jenny woke up startled. The night of the practical joke Roy played on her sprang into her mind again, someone was at the front door, trying to get into the house and the memories came flooding back.

For a few minutes she was fixed to the spot, her nerves jangling. She hadn't become fully awake and wasn't comprehending just what was happening. Then, there was loud shouting accompanied with banging on the door. Now she was fully awake and the voice was Roy's. He was shouting for her to let him in. Jenny pulled herself together and with some confusion, she opened the door to let him in. He stumbled over the step and made a grab for Jenny so as not to fall.

It was then she realised he was very drunk and although the front door wasn't locked, he somehow couldn't manage to open it. He had got himself into a right state, staggering all over the place and mumbling his words.

"Look at you…just look at you, why did you drink so much beer?" Jenny could feel anger rising in herself. "Sit down there and I'll make you some coffee to drink. You need to sober up a bit or you'll be in no fit state to report for duty tomorrow." She left him sitting on the sofa and went to the kitchen. Before she had time to make the coffee Roy was behind her, arms went round her waist, and he was nuzzling into her neck. "Get Off me!" she tried to push him away, "you stink of drink, and I don't want you kissing me!" She must have pushed him a bit too hard for as she turned around, he was on the floor struggling to get to his feet. When he was upright again, he suddenly lunged at Jenny and slapped her around her head.

"Don't shoo push me. I'll bash your face in, I'm a sh sh…sholdier an nobody pushes me" He lunged at her again and this time hit her on the side of the head with his fist.

Jenny reeled back startled at her husband's sudden violence. What had got into him? She knew he had a temper, but he had never, until now, raised a hand to her. Right now, all she could think about was to run from the room and shut herself in their bedroom placing a chair under the doorknob to stop him following her.

Flinging herself down on the bed, Jenny sobbed for a while until she stopped and suddenly jumped up from the bed as she thought of Amy. He wouldn't dare hurt her, would he? Without another thought she sprang into action and flung the chair to one side, opened the door, and ran to Amy's room. The child was sleeping peacefully but Jenny quickly picked her up and without hesitating ran back to her bedroom where she lay Amy in the middle of the bed. She then just as swiftly placed the chair back under the handle of the door.

There were no sounds coming from downstairs, so Jenny assumed that Roy had fallen asleep whether on the floor or the sofa, she really didn't care. She got on the bed next to her small daughter and snuggled up to her to try to go to sleep. Her mind was all over the place trying to work out why he had attacked her like that. His eyes had been glazed, and it was as though he hadn't realised who she was. They had argued a lot but never had she seen him so angry. The tears rolled down her cheeks once more and she held Amy even closer. Eventually she fell asleep.

CHAPTER 6

The next morning, after a very restless night, Jenny went downstairs with Amy in her arms. She placed the child in her highchair and went to look for Roy. He lay on the floor in the living room, his head underneath the coffee table in the middle of the room. He must have tried to take his shoes off because one was next to him and the other was hanging off his foot. Jenny went over to him and gently kicked him in his side to try to wake him. Nothing happened, so she bent down and gave him a big shake. This worked and he came to mumbling, "What's up, what d' you want? What time is it?" Jenny would have loved to just leave him there but knew he had to go to the barracks.

"Roy come on, get up, you need to wash and get yourself ready for duty." He appeared to have fallen asleep again, so Jenny kicked his foot until he woke again. This time he rose up quickly, but being half under the coffee table his head made contact with the wood. Jenny wanted to laugh. Serves him right she thought but instead she moved the table away from him so he could get up. He did get up this time whilst rubbing his sore head.

"What was that?" he demanded, "How the hell did I get under there?" He gave the table a shove and got to his feet with difficulty, but Jenny refused to help him and stood well away just in case he turned on her again. Without another word to him, she retreated back to the kitchen and proceeded to see to Amy's breakfast. She did, however, make Roy a cup of coffee, knowing that he would have one mighty hangover but other than that she decided it was not her fault and didn't want to speak to him. She still felt upset but also angry at his behaviour last night and really wanted to have it out with him but decided it would do no good until he was fully sober. So, until he left for the barracks, she would keep well away from him.

"Have we any Alka seltzer? I've got a terrible head on me this morning?" Roy, now dressed in army uniform, had entered the kitchen and was pulling open drawers and cupboard doors of the kitchen units.

"In that cupboard over there, the last one in the

row." Jenny did not want to look at him, it was as though he couldn't or wouldn't remember what had happened the night before. Surely he knew he had been at the pub drinking and as for afterwards, well, Jenny was astounded he was acting as if nothing happened. Not one sorry came from his lips! Without speaking again, Roy swallowed the fizzing drink, then quickly slurped down the cup of coffee and rushed to the front door and was gone, leaving all the drawers and cupboard doors open for Jenny to have to close again.

Later that day, although not in the mood at all, after visiting the shops and stopping at the park to give Amy a go on the swing, Jenny decorated the tree herself during Amy's nap.

She then poured herself a brandy, topped it up with lemonade and put her feet up. The drink went down well and she was tempted to have another one but no it wasn't wise, the one brandy had given her the courage to tackle Roy when he got home.

When five thirty came Jenny began to feel anxious. She was determined to speak with Roy and find answers to his behaviour. She tried keeping herself busy, giving Amy her tea and getting her ready for bedtime. Eventually the front door opened and in walked Roy. He did not speak but went straight upstairs to change out of his work uniform.

Huh! Jenny thought, not even a hello for her but then realised he was maybe avoiding her feeling shame for what he had done. Once he was sat in the armchair, Jenny spoke straight away fearing her courage might fail her if she waited any longer.

"Well Roy I would like an explanation of that behaviour you showed towards me last night!"

"What d'you want me to say? I got drunk and I know I shouldn't have, but I went to work didn't I, so what are you fussing for?" He sounded nonplussed at the questioning of him.

"Yes, you did get very drunk but what about your behaviour towards me when you finally came home?" Jenny knew Roy had been drunk, but she really wanted answers to why he was violent to her.

"What behaviour are you getting at? If you mean sleeping in here instead of coming upstairs to bed, well I must have dozed off after you went to bed."

Jenny was astounded, either her husband couldn't remember what he did to her or he was deliberately avoiding it, "Are you telling me that is all you can remember doing? What about becoming violent towards me? Haven't you got anything to say about that and perhaps an apology would be in order?"

Roy shifted his weight in the chair as though a sign he was becoming uncomfortable or embarrassed. "I don't remember being violent. I wouldn't do that but if I did and I'm not saying I did, it was probably too much beer that caused it."

"Well, I hope you never ever have too much beer again because I won't tolerate that sort of violent behaviour. I'm warning you Roy, that if it occurs again, I will be leaving you. D' you understand?" With that last remark Jenny went to the kitchen, put his tea on the table and then picking up Amy she went upstairs to put her to bed.

When she finally came down, Roy had finished his meal and said he was going to have a bath, then would have an early night and go straight to bed. Jenny settled on the sofa and picked up her book to read.

She was still annoyed that Roy had not said sorry for what had happened but knew there was no use talking to him about it now. She would just have to try to get over it and hope it never happened again. But what if it did happen again? She thought, would she carry out what she had warned him, and leave?

CHAPTER 7

Christmas Eve arrived and although Jenny and Roy were not yet fully speaking when her parents arrived, they both acted as though everything was just lovely and they were a happy little family. They all went out for a meal at the local pub. It was very busy and they had to wait a long time for their meals. When they did arrive, everyone eagerly ate the food and thoroughly enjoyed it. Amy became tired and was a little bit restless so after arriving back home she was soon asleep in her cot.

Christmas morning and Amy excitedly opened her presents. Tearing at the wrapping without needing encouragement but seemed to be more interested in playing with the boxes than the toys inside. Jenny's dad and Roy stayed with Amy and helped her play with the toys. The lunch went well though Betty had to help her daughter to get all the food cooked at the right times. Jenny's dad updated them about Tom, saying he was enjoying life in Germany but was coming to the end of his stay there and believed his next posting would be to Hong Kong but not sure exactly when. They wanted to know how Jenny and Roy were doing and were thrilled that Jenny had made two nice friends. After lunch Jenny's dad had a short nap which Betty explained he usually did after a large meal. The evening was occupied with playing Monopoly and having a few drinks to finish off the day.

Boxing Day was much the same except Jenny, Roy and Betty took Amy for a walk and called at the park which pleased Amy. Jenny also felt pleased that Roy had been his usual self and behaved very well to her parents. Her parents spent a lot of time with Amy acting as though they couldn't get enough of her and knowing they were leaving again to return to England and home the next day. That day came around all too quickly and Jenny and Roy went to the airport to wave her parents off on the plane. Leaving Jenny quite sad to see her parents leave but promising she would visit them at Easter.

On New Year's Eve there was another dance at the Barracks and Dave had agreed he would babysit

Amy if they wanted to go. Jenny agreed to go but only after Roy promised not to drink too much. After promising, they went to the dance. It was well past midnight and they had enjoyed seeing in the New Year. It had been a good evening, dancing and spending time with their friends and on returning home they started the New Year with another passionate night. Jenny appeared to have forgiven Roy for assaulting her but wouldn't forget it for a long time yet.

***

At the end of January, when Roy came home after a day of duty at the barracks, he announced that he was being posted to Germany and arrangements for him to fly out there were already in progress. Jenny was happy for him but had some trepidation about going up in an aeroplane. She told Roy this and he said it might be a while before she and Amy could join him there, similar to before having to wait to come to this camp.

"You mean I will have to fly to Germany by myself with Amy when the time comes to join you?"

"Well, yes, but you will be alright. I'm fairly sure you will be looked after." Roy told her with an air of confidence.

"Germany is a long way from here, isn't it?" Jenny's anxieties were beginning to show, and she had many questions for Roy. Mostly about not speaking the language, using different currency and could she take her belongings with her. Roy put his arms around her and told her not to worry about anything.

He promised to get the answers to her questions so when the time came for her to join him, she would know just what to expect. The following week Jenny's mind was in a whirl, but she calmed down a little after visiting Carol who was excited about her husband Kevin going to Germany also. So, Roy would still have Kevin as a friend, and this pleased Jenny. As for all those questions she had asked about going there, Carol did not have the answers either but reassured Jenny that they would probably be on the same flight out there together so they could support each other. This helped Jenny knowing she might not have to travel by herself with Amy.

Roy soon went off to Germany and once again Jenny was left on her own with Amy but this time, she couldn't just pop round to her mum for a chat. Nevertheless, she had Carol and Andrea who were both without their husbands and would sometimes chat the evening away at one or other of their homes while the children slept in another room. Her parents also visited her very often and on one such visit Betty brought her sewing machine telling Jenny she could keep it and do some dressmaking to pass the time. Jenny had been so grateful for the machine and started immediately making a skirt for herself after her parents left to return home.

Into February, Jenny realised her period was late but tried not to worry believing all the stress and anxiety could be to blame. However, when March arrived and still no appearance of a period she began to wonder if there was another reason for this. On the next visit from her mum, Jenny confided in her and she suggested that if one more was missed then Jenny should visit the doctor. Nothing happened and by now Jenny had remembered the passionate night after the New Year dance and so became convinced that what she had suspected must be true. The doctor confirmed that Jenny was indeed pregnant and Jenny questioned him about flying out to Germany while being pregnant. The doctor assured Jenny that if she were healthy then it would be ok but perhaps not until after three months and certainly not the last couple of weeks before her due date of expected birth.

Jenny was in a quandary, should she Join Roy and risk flying or wait until the baby had been born. She was certain Roy would want her to join him just as soon as she was able, but he would not want to wait another six months. Her parents on the other hand, when they were told of the pregnancy, wanted Jenny to go back home to live with them until after the birth.

She really wanted to be with her husband but remembering the night he was violent after getting drunk, her mind was fixed on the consequences if that were to happen again whilst she was pregnant.

In the end she brushed aside that memory believing she could trust Roy not to do that again and decided to join him whenever accommodation had been allocated to them.

***

Roy was delighted to know they were expecting another child saying it would be perfect because by the time it was born Amy would be two and she would be happy also to have a little brother or sister. So as the weeks passed, Jenny was happy that she had made the right decision but was now eager to fly out to Germany.

Roy wrote to her when she was almost five months pregnant to inform her they had been allocated a flat and that Jenny would be provided with the necessary documents, flight times and tickets in the next two weeks. Her parents had already helped her to pack belongings in two wooden crates supplied by the army and she was now packing clothes and a few toys into a large suitcase ready for the journey.

Her parents were to accompany her to a location in London where her documents would be checked and she would assemble with others travelling on the same flight. Jenny was allocated a soldier to look after her and Amy, both at the airport and on the aeroplane until Roy was to meet her at the German airport. There was no sign of Carol or Andrea, so she guessed they were on a different flight.

Everything went well, the soldier named Ben carried Amy onto the plane and sat on the other side of the aisle from Jenny. She was very nervous with not knowing what to expect and as the plane took off Ben reached across and held her hand. The rest of the journey went ok and they were soon landing at the airport where, as soon as Amy saw her daddy, she ran up to him for a big hug. Roy said he was pleased they had finally arrived there and he patted his wife's stomach with a big grin on his face. There was another soldier waiting for them with Roy. He introduced him to Jenny. It was Colin's car and even had a baby seat for Amy which Colin explained was his son's.

It was about an hour's car journey from the airport to the army camp, but Jenny hardly noticed the scenery because Roy chatted nonstop. When they arrived, all Jenny could see were huge buildings, some with windows and others looked like large garages. The accommodation was in a block of flats, just outside the main barracks. Their flat was on the second floor and looked out towards the barracks and thankfully there was a lift. Once settled in, Roy thanked Colin and then made a cup of tea for Jenny. The flat was nicely decorated and the furniture, although very plain, was adequate. Roy had prepared everything. There were groceries in the kitchen and even the bed was made up as well as Amy's cot. He had also hired a television, so Jenny was more than pleased with his effort to make her welcome.

The following morning was Saturday, so Roy was

at home. He offered to show Jenny around the area so she would not get lost when on her own. Jenny liked what she could see. There was a large grocery store which Roy told her was the NAAFI and a short way from that was a place to have coffee with a small shop selling bits and bobs called the TOC H. Strange names for the buildings, but Roy explained these were army ones and not German shops. The following weekend, Roy took Jenny into the town and showed her around the shops there.

They ended their tour in a huge shop selling everything from food to furniture and Roy explained that there were many such stores in Germany because it was normal to be able to buy everything in one place. These, he explained, were called Hypermarkets.

Jenny made a friend in the flat opposite and her name was Renata. She was a German girl married to a British soldier. Renata agreed to teach Jenny some basic phrases she might need if she went shopping in the town. Renata had two children, a seven-month baby boy and a three-year-old daughter. She also took her to the health centre where Jenny would have antenatal check-ups. Renata was a trained nurse offering to drive Jenny to the hospital when her labour started, though Jenny thought that unnecessary as she would call an ambulance.

When relating this to Roy, he told her that he was being taught to drive, a requirement by the army so he could drive army vehicles and, after he was qualified, he possibly might buy a used car. If this happened soon then he would be able to take her to the hospital. Jenny felt safe in the knowledge that she may have two people she could rely on when the birth was due. Though this didn't stop her anxieties of having the birth occurring in a hospital where they spoke a different language. Would she be able to communicate with them there?

***

Over the next few months Jenny got more used to being in a foreign country. She wrote often to her parents and they were delighted when told Amy could now speak many words and also that Jenny could speak some German.

There were also visits from army people to see how she had settled in. One such visit was from the padre of Roy's regiment and the other was the SSAFA sister, a forces welfare nurse who had been allocated to

Jenny because she was pregnant. With only weeks to the due date, there was concern that Jenny's blood pressure was high and it was suggested that if it remained high over the next week, Jenny should be admitted to hospital for observation until the baby was born.

Hospitalisation was necessary and Roy was given compassionate leave to look after Amy. Jenny found there were some staff members who spoke English, so this eased her anxieties. A baby boy was born to her a week later. They named him Charlie after Roy's father and all went well. Jenny was discharged to go home and Roy collected her and baby Charlie in the second-hand car which he had purchased from another soldier. Amy was so happy to meet her baby brother and could not stop stroking his head.

The following weeks were a mix of visits from friends, the SSAFA sister and Jenny's parents who flew out the week after Charlie was born. Trying to get into some semblance of a routine was very difficult. Charlie was not such a contented baby as Amy had been and suffering from colic, he kept his parents on their toes. This lasted for a month and then Charlie began to settle at last and Jenny was able to get into some sort of routine. Renata had been a Godsend and could settle Charlie better than any of them. Jenny was so grateful to have her as a friend.

***

As the weeks went by Jenny was able to enjoy having two children to look after and her friendship with Renata grew much closer. They visited the park together and the cafe for a coffee. She had got used to seeing soldiers around with tanks and jeeps travelling on the roads around the camp. There was just one thing that she was a bit concerned about. There was a troop bar in the barracks and Roy had taken to frequenting this with his army mates. It was not every day but was becoming more frequent, maybe two or three times a week. It was usually after finishing work and for maybe an hour, but Jenny could not relax on the days he visited the bar. Eventually, one evening Jenny brought up the subject of him drinking and Roy simply shrugged.

"I enjoy having some time with the lads, it helps to cope with the work we have to do."

"Why can't you just go at the weekend, and I could come with you? Since Charlie arrived you haven't taken me out at all."

"Well, you seem so wrapped up in the baby and Amy when I get home in the evening, I didn't think you wanted to go out."

"It does take up a lot of my time getting both our children fed and ready for bed. A little help from you would help, but you don't seem to show any interest in feeding Charlie and Amy must play by herself while I am busy."

"Oh, so now you are blaming me for not having enough time to be able to go out enjoying yourself. Don't you think I get tired after all day at the barracks and deserve a rest when I get home."

"Yes, but they are your children as well as mine, but it seems to me that I am the only one looking after them. Why don't you show more interest in them is all I'm asking?"

At this point in the conversation, Roy got upset and his voice rising he shouted at Jenny, "What do you expect of me? I work and earn money to keep you and the kids. It is your job to look after the kids and I just want some peace and quiet when I get home."

Jenny was taken aback at his reaction and words. He had never said this to her and she couldn't believe he felt like this. All she was asking was just a little help now and again. She worked hard keeping the house clean and tidy, shopping, cooking and looking after Charlie and Amy. Didn't Roy realise that she got tired as well as getting fed up with the everyday routine?

A night out would be lovely, but Roy didn't appear to care about her well being. She did not speak again for the rest of the evening but could feel resentment building up in her about what Roy had said.

CHAPTER 8

For the rest of that week, conversation between Jenny and Roy was quite subdued. Roy didn't go to the bar at the barracks, instead returning home on time where he did play with Amy for a while and also got her ready for bed on some evenings. He still didn't have much to do with Charlie which was puzzling Jenny. Whilst visiting Renata she confided in her about Roy's attitude towards Charlie and hoped she could come up with an explanation as to Roy's behaviour.

"Perhaps Roy resents not having your attention now that Charlie takes up most of your time."

"Yes, but he must realise that looking after another child would keep me busier which is not my fault if I don't have time to fuss over Roy," Jenny replied in her defence.

"Well, would it be possible to put Charlie to bed

before Roy got home, then only having Amy to see to would give you more time to talk with Roy?"

Jenny thought over what Renata had suggested and replied "Oh, I could give that a try, starting with today. Thanks Renata, your suggestion has been helpful."

"I could be even more helpful if you agree with what I am about to say."

"Oh, what might that be?" Jenny was interested to know what her friend had in mind.

"My daughter has been going to the kindergarten based in the camp since she was two for three days a week."

"The kindergarten, what's that I haven't heard of that. Is it something just for children?"

"It is a playgroup for children from two to five year olds. It is only for the morning and if you would like to send Amy there, I could take them both in the morning and pick them up again at lunchtime."

"Oh, I don't really know. Amy has never been parted from me or Roy and I am not sure if she would get on all right there. Not being three yet"

"Why not give it a try? She will be with Eva, and she knows her and likes playing with her. I could take you there tomorrow and you could enrol Amy. Perhaps if you stay with her for an hour she will get used to being there."

"Alright, I will give it some thought and speak to Roy to get his opinion on this and if all is ok, I will call in the morning to go to this Kinder… what did you call it?"

"It's kindergarten. That is what they call playschool here in Germany."

They parted company with much for Jenny to think about. She liked the idea of having three mornings free from looking after Amy, so she was willing if only Roy would agree.

That evening Charlie was in bed fast asleep and Amy was already in her nightclothes. Jenny thought it would be a clever idea for her, Roy and Amy to have tea all together. Jenny waited and waited for Roy. It was now two hours since he should have been home. Amy had her tea and was now in her bed. The nice tea

Jenny had prepared for Roy was now ruined.

She kept a lookout at the window to check if she could see her husband coming. There was no sight of him and Jenny began to wonder if something bad had happened. She needn't have worried because an hour later she saw him crossing the road and what's more he appeared to be staggering. Jenny's immediate thought was that he must be drunk. It had been such a while since he had been drunk so why now?

She sat down on the sofa, picked up a magazine to pretend all was normal and she wasn't anxious. Roy came into the house none too quietly. He stood in the doorway to the living room just staring at Jenny. When she could stand it no longer, she turned to face him.

"So, where have you been? I was worried something had happened to you, but I see you have been drinking with your army mates again!"

Roy didn't answer her immediately but just kept staring. He had the glazed eyes look again and Jenny was becoming nervous. "So, there is no need to tell you, I've been having a drink with my mates and now I'm home for my tea."

Jenny didn't like the tone of his voice, it had a threatening sound about it and not wanting to antagonise him, she got up and moved to go past him saying, "Your tea was ruined. I had it ready ages ago. Thought you, me and Amy could have tea together but not to worry, I'll get something else ready for you if you let me pass to go to the kitchen."

As Jenny approached, he stood to one side so she could pass but as she reached the doorway, he grabbed her arm and in a menacing tone he spoke, "I'm the boss in this house, not you and don't you ever tell me I can't go for a drink with my mates at the barracks!" He then pushed Jenny through the door, "Now get in that kitchen and get me some tea, I'm starving."

Jenny went to the kitchen and began to prepare food for Roy, but a few minutes later he followed her and seeing what she was preparing he said, "I don't want that, you can find something else, especially something more substantial to feed a soldier."

"Well, if you can tell me what you want, I will get it for you," Jenny was doing her best to be nice to him, but it didn't seem to be working."

"That's just it, you never seem to know what I

want. You're too wrapped up in the kids to bother about me. It's only when I go drinking that I get your attention."

"That's not true. The children take up a lot of my time, but in the evening, you don't want to talk and are too tired and so go to bed early." Jenny tried to explain the way things were.

This appeared to make Roy angrier. He grabbed both her arms tightly and pushed her backwards so she slammed into the worktop. Then, raising his hand, he slapped her around the head several times.

When he stopped slapping her, he said angrily, "That's because I've nothing to talk to you about. You never ask me what sort of day I've had, it's just you going on about Charlie doing this or Amy said that. I would like some attention like you give our kids." With that he let go of Jenny who pushed him hard so she could get past him and run upstairs to the bedroom. Once inside the room, she placed a chair under the doorknob as she had done once before. This time though, Roy had followed her and tried to push the door open. When the door held fast shut, he banged on the door shouting "That's it run and hide and don't stay to hear me out." Jenny curled up on the bed and wished he would go away. She was shaking and tears welled up in her eyes.

After several minutes, she heard him go back downstairs so she relaxed a little while listening out for any sounds from the children. All was quiet, so she assumed his shouting had not woken them up. She must have eventually fallen asleep because when she woke it was daylight. The clock on the bedside table showed it was six, so she made herself get up and go to the bathroom for a shower. She knew she wouldn't be disturbed by Roy but just in case, she locked the door behind her. She had just finished dressing when she heard Amy talking to Charlie. So, going into them, she lifted Charlie and told Amy to follow her downstairs.

Jenny still felt shaken after last night but realised Roy would have sobered up and he didn't appear to show his temper except after lots of beer. He was asleep on the sofa, so she told Amy not to disturb him but follow her into the kitchen. Amy obeyed and took a seat at the table. It was just as she was finishing feeding Charlie when Roy appeared in the doorway looking very dishevelled. He spoke after several minutes standing there, "I'm sorry for last night, Jenny. Will you forgive me? I promise it will never happen again."

She did not answer straight away but instead finished seeing to Charlie, "You said that the last time it happened and so I don't believe you will keep your promise, especially if you go drinking straight from work."

"I do mean it this time, please believe me. I know it is the drink which makes me aggressive so I must learn to control myself. I love you and hate myself for hurting you. I really am very sorry."

"Well, if you ever do this again then like I said before, I will leave and go back to England where I know me and the children will be safe." Jenny found the courage to warn him once again and in her mind, she meant what she said.

***

For several months, Roy was on his best behaviour. He appeared to be keeping his promise and came home at once after work. Charlie was six months old and sitting on the floor, he loved Amy to play with him and his toys. Jenny made an extra effort to have the children ready for bed by the time Roy came home and he read them stories before bedtime. She also made a fuss of Roy when they were alone, remembering to ask him how his day had been. On one such evening while they chatted, Roy mentioned he was probably going away for two weeks on an exercise. Jenny showed an interest in this and asked her husband what that entailed. He explained that these exercises were to train the soldiers in combat with the enemy and could be in open fields or in forests. It was all a matter of what the training included. She asked a lot of questions and Roy seemed pleased she was interested.

A week later, the exercise began and once more, Jenny found herself on her own with the children. This time, however, she felt relieved Roy was absent because she could relax and not worry that he might get drunk again. Amy had been attending kindergarten for two months now and after taking her there, Jenny walked home with Renata and they occasionally called at the TOC H for coffee. The days with Roy away seemed more pleasant for Jenny. She had more time to herself and being relaxed, started sewing again, this time making Amy a Sundress. The two weeks went by all too quickly and Roy returned home again to the delight of Amy who had drawn several pictures at kindergarten and she couldn't wait to show her daddy.

Jenny had decided to try to ask him all about the exercise and kept what she had been up to quiet, only mentioning it if Roy asked her. Family life got back on track again and Roy even took Jenny to the troop bar where she enjoyed chatting with the other wives there, but all the while conscious of what Roy was drinking. She didn't need to worry because her husband was on his best behaviour… but would this last?

CHAPTER 9

It was a week later. Jenny and the children were waiting for Roy to get home at 5.30 when a loud knock on the front door startled her. Standing outside were two soldiers whom Jenny recognised by the red band on their arms as being the military police.

"Good evening, Mrs Crabtree, we are here to tell you that your husband will not be home this evening because he had a fight with another soldier." She was told politely. Jenny was shocked by this information but even more surprised when the soldier continued. "He has been retained and will spend the night in a cell at the guardroom and will face his commanding officer in the morning to be disciplined. If all goes well, he will be home tomorrow evening." He smiled and then asked if she would be ok and was there anything they could do for her.

Jenny could not speak for a moment, then she began to question the men, "Is he hurt and had he been drinking and is the other soldier all right?" The words just tumbled out of her mouth, showing how shocked she was.

"Neither your husband nor the other person involved are badly hurt and yes, your husband had been drinking heavily in the local pub after the day's duties which is where the fight took place. We are deeply sorry to bring you this news and we hope you will be ok until your husband comes home."

"Thank you for coming to tell me, it is a bit of a shock, but I will be ok and can only hope my husband will return home tomorrow evening." With those last words they said their goodbyes and left.

Roy returned home the next evening but wouldn't discuss anything, just saying once again that he was sorry it had happened. Jenny was cross with him and told him he was always saying sorry, but it was just a word and he didn't mean it. The rest of that week they hardly spoke to each other. Roy appeared to be in a sulky mood and Jenny remained angry with him. She later found out from Renata that Roy had been given a warning, told to manage his drinking habit and was put on cleaning duties for a week. None of this came from Roy who still refused to discuss what had taken place or his punishment from the commanding officer.

She had every right to be angry with him behaving the way he had and a week later she was yet again hearing him say sorry. He came home late and drunk. They argued and this time he pushed her so hard that she ended up on the floor, hitting her arm on a cupboard as she fell. This resulted in a large bruise appearing the next day. It was just coincidental that on that afternoon, the SSAFA sister called to check on her. She had been informed of the fighting incident at the pub involving her husband a week ago and wanted to make sure Jenny and the children were ok. Any other time, she would have found Jenny a smiley cheerful mother but instead Jenny was morose and a visitor was the last thing she wanted.

With tea and biscuits on the coffee table, Jenny tried to be nice but when Amy reached for a biscuit without asking, it was with sharp words, she told her to wait and mind her manners. The SSAFA sister responded kindly when the young child began to cry and smiling, she asked Amy to sit on her lap. She then asked her if she would like a biscuit and Amy said "yes, please", so the biscuit was given to her and whilst she nibbled on it, she remained on the SSAFA sister's knee quite content, her tears forgotten. Jenny apologised for her lack of patience giving an excuse of tiredness but saying that was no excuse for intolerance towards her daughter.

"You look tired and if I may say so, also looking quite sad. Are you feeling all right or is something bothering you that you might like to talk to me about? I can assure you that it would be in confidence should you share your troubles."

Jenny was silent when suddenly tears welled up and spilled out over her cheeks. The SSAFA sister just sat silent until Jenny's crying had subsided. She then told Amy she would love a drawing like the ones she did at kindergarten and asked her to go sit at the kitchen table and draw a picture for her. As soon as Amy had gone, the SSAFA sister asked Jenny again if she wanted to talk. Slowly Jenny began to tell her all about Roy and his behaviour, finally ending by saying how anxious and frightened she was becoming. The SSAFA sister rose and went over to sit next to Jenny and gently put an arm around her. "Oh, my dear, I am sorry to hear about your troubles. I could tell you were sad about something. Has this been going on for long?"

"The first time, Roy got angry and gave me just a slap. That was back in England, but he promised it wouldn't happen again. Then after Charlie was born, he began coming home late after drinking at the troop bar in the camp. It is then, after the beer, that he becomes angry and violent." Her tears came again and the SSAFA sister waited patiently to speak but kept her arm around Jenny comforting her.

"This can't be allowed to continue but what to do about it. It sounds to me that your husband has some issues he is not dealing with and maybe he needs to talk to someone about them. Does he ever hit the children when he has been drinking?"

"No. Amy and Charlie are in bed by the time he eventually arrives home. Also, if he were to go upstairs angry, I would protect them from him, but I feel sure he wouldn't harm them. D'you think it's my fault he is like this? He says I don't give him enough attention but even when I have tried this, he still drinks and gets violent.

"No. You mustn't blame yourself. You are a good

mother and wife so something else is driving him to be like this. If he ever shows the slightest violence to the children as well as yourself, please leave the house with them and come to the safety of the barracks. Will you do this for me?

"Of course I would do that and I told him if it happened again, I would go back to England. All he says to me is sorry, but this is meaningless because he then does it again. Now, I am feeling anxious every day waiting to see if he arrives home at five thirty. I don't want to have to go back to England. Do you think the army will fly me and the children there if the situation comes to that?"

I'm afraid perhaps they cannot do that because it would appear they are encouraging you to leave your husband. Let me see what the situation is about providing a flight for someone suffering abuse such as you have told me about."

"Oh please don't tell his commanding officer about my situation. I feel it would just make things worse if he were to reprimand Roy and I don't want my husband to know I have been talking about this to anyone."

"Then I will visit you several times a week to check on you. Do not mention this to your husband, he doesn't need to know. Can you talk to your parents about what is happening? Maybe they will be willing to help in some way. Now try to cheer up if only for the children's sake, I am here for you and will support you as much as you need."

"Thank you, that is so kind but if it does happen again then I will find a way to go back to England. I cannot let me or my children live in a violent home."

The SSAFA sister reminded her again to try to be cheerful for the children's sake and said she would see Jenny again in two days. With that she said goodbye to Amy and Charlie, telling Amy she would be back for her picture and with a pat on Jenny's arm she left.

***

The sister kept her promise and visited Jenny often. Amy was always happy to see her telling Jenny she liked the sister very much. As the weeks passed, Jenny began to believe that Roy had learnt his lesson and was indeed keeping his promise not to drink at the troop bar. Although Jenny was not to know that he was hiding some resentment towards her for not wanting him to meet his army mates, he had realised though, that he could not risk losing her if his violent behaviour continued. He was still having a drink at lunchtimes in the local pub just a short way from the barracks but was so far keeping his drinking under control.

This secrecy was more for himself than anyone else. After the bar fight, the commanding officer had warned him that if he didn't keep his drinking under control then he would have no alternative but to dismiss him from the army for bad conduct.

Jenny did not inform her parents of her troubles, but the next letter Jenny received from her parents was to tell her they were coming to visit the following week. They would just be staying for the weekend and wondered if Roy could pick them up at the airport. Jenny felt happy that her parents would be visiting and when telling Amy, she was so excited to be seeing her Grandparents. However, later when she told Roy, he was not so happy and suggested to Jenny that she might like to put them off visiting. She told Roy she wouldn't do that and both she and the children wanted them to visit.

Roy began arguing with Jenny, trying to change

her mind and when she wouldn't do as he had asked, he stormed out of the house, leaving Jenny wondering what his motive had been for his request to her.

She spent the evening trying not to think about what mood he would be in when he got back. She had first thought he had just been going for a walk but, as the hours passed, she started to wonder if he had gone to the troop bar. This made her anxious as to whether he would be drunk and lead to him being violent again. Surely, she thought, he wouldn't risk getting drunk again after all these weeks. Jenny had her answer when on hearing the front door open, Roy almost stumbled into the room.

He flopped down onto the sofa and in a menacing voice spoke to Jenny, "Yes as you can see, I have been drinking, so what are you going to do about it, tell my commanding officer?"

Jenny took a deep breath and replied, "I'm not going to do anything, I don't even want to speak to you and I am going to bed." When she got up to leave the room, Roy jumped up and grabbed her pushing her down onto the sofa. "Leave me alone you bully. I won't stand for you hurting me!" Jenny, although trembling and frightened, was not going to just let him hurt her.

"Oh, little wifey has a voice," he laughingly said, "what you going to do, call the police like you did before when you couldn't take a joke?"

Jenny tried to push him away to get up and leave, but he wouldn't move. "Why are you like this? You act as though you hate me and I have done nothing to make you be like this."

"Oh, you have done nothing! You really have no idea have you? Just how humiliated I felt when you had to go and call the police on me. Your loving husband and you couldn't take a practical joke. Now I am making something of myself, but your parents still hate me and you think I would be pleased to have them visit us." Roy almost spat out the last words and his glazed eyes looked wild as he stared menacingly at her.

After what seemed like ages he moved away from Jenny and she saw her opportunity to leave. She wasn't quick enough though and he grabbed her arm, pulling her back, he then flung her across the room, hitting her side as she plummeted to the floor. Jenny lay there trembling and didn't dare to move. Roy leaned over her with a threatening look and began pummelling her with his fists. Jenny tried to cover her face but still a few blows smashed into her and then she could feel the trickle of wetness down over her top lip and guessed her nose was now bleeding. He eventually stopped and left the room, but Jenny still didn't try to get up. She wanted to make sure he had really gone before trying to make her escape to the bedroom.

Eventually, she got up and made a dash for the stairs. Once she reached the safety of the bedroom and had secured the chair under the door handle, she began to cry. This was the worst she thought and was afraid the violence was getting out of hand, but what was she to do? Her next thought was for the children so, although she was afraid, she somehow found courage to go to their room and again placing a chair to secure the door, she curled up on the floor and prayed that Roy would calm down and go to sleep. Tomorrow she would go to see the SSAFA sister and demand that the army keep her husband away from her and the children while she made arrangements to fly back to England.

CHAPTER 10

The next morning, after a very restless and painful night, Jenny decided to stay in the children's bedroom and keep Amy there with her. Amy wanted to know why her mummy had slept in her room and could see that her mummy had been hurt. She touched Jenny's face under her eye causing her mummy to wince with pain. Jenny did not want to lie to her daughter but also didn't want to tell her that daddy did it. So, she made up a story that she had tripped on the stairs, bumping her head and because daddy was already asleep, she didn't want to disturb him so she thought it would be a good idea to sleep with her and Charlie. Amy accepted this but then announced she was thirsty and wanted her breakfast. Jenny thought for a few minutes then suggested Amy get washed and dressed ready for kindergarten to save time as they were already upstairs and near the bathroom. Amy didn't protest and trundled off to do as her mummy suggested.

Jenny listened intently for any movement downstairs, realising she couldn't stay upstairs for much longer. Just as Amy came back into the room, Jenny heard the front door bang and assumed that was Roy going to the barracks. It was seven thirty and was about the time he usually left. As soon as Amy was dressed, Jenny picked up Charlie, wincing in pain from her side as she did so and they all proceeded to go downstairs. In the kitchen she gave Charlie his breakfast and Amy sat at the table to eat her cereal. As soon as breakfast was over, Jenny quickly dressed Charlie and they all set off for the kindergarten. Amy chatted all the way there and she happily ran inside to see her friends. Jenny tried to hide her swollen face as much as she could and luckily there wasn't anyone close enough to see it.

Although Jenny had tried keeping her mind off what Roy did, she was now full of anxieties about what she was about to do. At the barrack gates, she enquired of the soldier on guard duty where she might locate the SSAFA sister's office, all the while hoping the makeup she had put on earlier was disguising her black eye. He was very polite to Jenny when telling her that he would telephone through to the barracks to get someone to show her where to go. Charlie had fallen asleep and after waiting about ten minutes, a young soldier arrived and asked her to follow him. Without saying any further words, they arrived at the office she needed. Jenny thanked him for helping her and the soldier left her standing outside the office door.

Hesitantly, Jenny knocked on the door. There was no answer, so she knocked harder and a female voice inside urged her to come in. Inside she found a young female soldier sitting at a desk. This wasn't the SSAFA sister who had been visiting her and Jenny became even more nervous.

"Hello, can I help you?" The young woman greeted Jenny, introducing herself at the same time. The girl physically winced at the sight of Jenny's face.

"I..., I'm looking for the SSAFA sister. I..., I need to speak to her urgently." Jenny's voice showed her nervousness.

"The SSAFA sister has gone out on her morning rounds of visiting and won't be back until lunchtime. Would you like to leave a message and I will see that she gets it?"

This nonplussed Jenny and she could feel what

little courage she had was now diminishing fast. "Well, would she be able to visit me early this afternoon? I really need to speak with her. It's about the abuse we have talked about and I really do need her help please." Jenny could feel the tears threatening to spill over, but she tried hard not to cry in front of this young girl.

Spotting the blackening of Jenny's eye and noting how upset she was, she realised this must be urgent. The girl asked for Jenny's name saying she would get in touch with sister and Jenny could expect a visit later that morning if Jenny would be at home. She replied she would be there and gave her name and not wanting to stay any longer she thanked her and proceeded to leave, then hesitated and asked if her address was also needed, to which the girl answered that it would not be needed just her name would be sufficient.

Jenny returned home and restlessly waited to see if the sister would call. Remembering that Amy would need to be collected from kindergarten, she reluctantly went to see Renata to ask for her help in collecting Amy. Her friend was only too happy to do this and spotting the black eye Renata asked Jenny if everything was all right. "Did Roy do that to your eye?" she asked bluntly.

Jenny had forgotten that Renata might see her eye, but it was difficult lying to her friend, "We had an argument, but I tripped and fell banging the side of my face on the coffee table."

"Are you sure that is really what happened or are you covering for him? I know he has been violent before because you told me so?"

At this point Jenny burst into tears and the whole truth came tumbling out including that she was expecting a visit from the SSAFA sister to discuss what to do about Roy's behaviour. She stopped herself from revealing that she was thinking of leaving and going back to England. Nothing was in place to enable her to do that yet, so Jenny kept this to herself for now.

"Oh no, Jenny I am so sorry for you. He is a beast and doesn't deserve you!" Then Renata surprised Jenny by saying, "Give Charlie to me. I will look after him and Amy after I collect her and will give them some lunch with my children. Don't worry I will tell them it is a special treat and I am sure they will like that."

Jenny was so grateful, and she accepted the offer of help straight away and after hugging her friend she went to get the pushchair for Charlie.

At eleven thirty the SSAFA sister arrived and Jenny was more than happy to see her. Immediately she noticed Jenny's face and suggested Jenny should sit down and tell her what had happened.

Jenny related everything about the evening before, starting with the argument over her parents impending visit and ending where she spent the night in the children's room to protect them and herself from harm.

"Are you ok now? Has he hurt you anywhere besides your face?" The sister sounded very concerned.

"My side is a bit sore and bruised from where I hit it on the corner of the coffee table before landing face down on the floor."

"I would like to see your side for myself. May I have a look?" Sister was looking concerned.

"Of course, but it doesn't hurt too much." Jenny proceeded to lift her top up so the sister could look where it was hurting.

"Oh, dear you have a large bruise I'm afraid. He really has treated you violently, I must say."

"By the way, where are your two children? I haven't heard them." The SSAFA sister suddenly noticed the absence of Charlie and Amy.

"Amy is at kindergarten for the morning and Charlie is being looked after by my friend Renata and she should be collecting Amy right about now. Then she is giving them their lunch before I pick them up this afternoon."

"Did your husband hurt the children in any way?

"Oh no, they slept right through it all, even when I stayed in their room, so they aren't hurt at all." Jenny was quick to reassure the SSAFA sister."

"Amy accepted the excuse I gave her as to why mummy slept in her bedroom, so she wouldn't realise what had happened." Jenny was adamant to let the sister know her children were being looked after. The last thing she needed was to have her children taken into care.

"Right now, what do you want to do? How can I best help you? This violence from your husband cannot be allowed to continue. Somehow, I must make sure you and the children are kept safe."

"That is kind of you to want to help and I would like my husband to be kept away from us if that is possible?"

"Of course, that is exactly what I was thinking but you must know that in order to do that, I must report the situation to your husband's commanding officer. Also, it would be a good idea to visit the hospital to make sure the assault is recorded and to make sure that you are ok."

Jenny was lost in thought for a few minutes then she came to a decision. "If that must be done to keep us safe then go ahead and do whatever you must do. I have made up my mind that when my parents visit in a week's time, I shall be returning to England with them."

The SSAFA sister looked surprised at Jenny's decision. She was hoping that an enforced separation for a few weeks while things could be sorted out and Roy would agree to stop drinking would solve this matter for Jenny. However, she understood how frightened Jenny must be and did not want her to be hurt again.

"Are you sure that is the action you want to take? Would you not consider holding back from leaving while I see if somehow, I can prevent your husband from doing this by changing his behaviour?"

"No, I have made up my mind. He has had enough chances, always saying he is sorry, and it won't happen again, but it always does, he'll never change. So, I'm afraid sorry isn't enough anymore"

"You must do whatever you think is best for you and the children. Have you already told your parents about this and your intention to return with them?"

"I haven't had time to warn them yet. I'll go and phone just as soon after you leave me."

"Your parents will be visiting in a week, you say. That is such a short time to prepare to leave. Packing up your belongings will need to be done and flight arrangements to be made. Then there is the problem of who will pay for your flight. I'm afraid the army will not finance this because they could be accused of causing you to separate from your husband."

"Don't concern yourself about that. I'm sure when he knows the situation and predicament I am in, my father will cover the expense of a plane ticket for me and the children. But whether I can get on the same flight as them, that remains to be seen. I'll know more after I have spoken to him."

"Well then, if you are sure that is what you want to do then can you come back to the barracks with me? You can telephone from my office while I go and speak to the commanding officer. I shall make sure you are back here to collect your children, but can I suggest you inform your friend so she will know your whereabouts. First though I will take you to the emergency department at the hospital and get you seen as quickly as possible.".

Jenny accepted the help suggested to her and the sister waited while she went to speak to Renata. Her friend had only just got back from kindergarten and was eager to know what the SSAFA sister and Jenny had discussed.

Jenny promised Renata that she would tell her everything when she came for the children later but she did not have time just now. Jenny kissed Charlie and Amy, telling them to be good for Renata, then she left to join the SSAFA sister in her car. They set off for the hospital which was in the town just a few miles from the camp.

At the hospital, the SSAFA sister reported to the receptionist and requested that Jenny be seen urgently. Whatever she had said, Jenny was ushered into an office from the waiting room immediately. A young army doctor made notes on what Jenny told him and inspected her face and bruised side. After having her face and side x-rayed, he told Jenny there were no broken bones and would recover but she needed to rest and take some pain relief. He then asked her if she would allow him to send his report about her injuries to Roy's Commanding Officer so he would have all the facts on the assault by her husband. Jenny hesitated but was assured by the SSAFA sister that it would be best to let the doctor do this. So, it was agreed that the doctor could send a report.

CHAPTER 11

Jenny had made the phone call to her parents and was now awaiting the return of the SSAFA sister. She did not have to wait long until the sister came back. She told Jenny that the Commanding Officer would like to see her. This was a surprise that he should want to speak with her, but she agreed to go if the sister would be there with her.

Jenny did not expect to see a younger but distinguished looking man sitting behind a desk. He couldn't be much older than her and was quite handsome. This made Jenny feel uneasy; she had expected that Roy's commanding officer would be a much older man. He stood up as she entered and promptly shook hands introducing himself and indicating with his other hand that she should sit facing him.

"Well now Mrs Crabtree, sister has informed me of the upset you are having with your husband and I wanted to meet you to let you know how sorry I am to learn of you suffering violent abuse from your husband. I must say I am surprised to hear this. Private Crabtree is an exemplary soldier and after my chat to discipline him for fighting with another soldier I believed he has been on his best behaviour." There was a pause then the Officer spoke again. "I will do my utmost to help along with sister of course. It must be very distressing for you to have your husband misbehaving in this way and I can understand your anxiety. Please tell me how you would most like me to help you resolve this."

Jenny cleared her throat and although feeling nervous told the officer, "I want you to keep my husband away from me and the children, perhaps keep him living at the barracks. I have now spoken to my parents who have a planned visit at the end of next week and have told them that I want to return to England with them after their visit. My father has agreed to make all the arrangements necessary. This would put myself and the children at a safe distance while I decide what my future should be with my husband."

The officer listened intently to her explanation and told Jenny that he could certainly confine her husband to reside in the barracks and he would most definitely be reprimanded. He also asked Jenny to rethink her plans to go home with her parents, instead suggesting she give himself and the sister a chance to resolve her problems.

Jenny thanked him for his kindness and the offer to keep Roy at the barracks, but she was adamant to go home and have time in safety to think about what her next move would be. The commanding officer asked if she knew what her plans were regarding her marriage, pointing out that he hoped it would not end in divorce. He then advised her that a divorce was a long-drawn-out process and to think very carefully if that were the route she would take.

He asked Jenny to please keep the SSAFA sister informed of her decisions after returning to England. Jenny promised she would do that stating the sister had been such an enormous help to her. After leaving his office, the SSAFA sister promised she would visit Jenny every day and then gave her phone number stating she could ring her anytime even just to chat.

At home, Jenny's first thoughts were to collect

Amy and Charlie. Renata was so pleased to see her and immediately wanted to know all about Jenny's day. Jenny related all that had happened that day, including her visit with Roy's commanding officer.

Renata was amazed about Jenny getting to see him. She wanted to know if he would help and Jenny told her that Roy would be confined to barracks not able to leave there at any time, so there would be no danger of seeing him. Renata showed some concern and told Jenny that if he came to see her, she must come to her flat with the children for safety.

Later that evening, Jenny felt exhausted and the realisation of what was happening caused the tears to flow again. She had a long cry and afterwards felt less stressed. After some supper, she checked that the doors were securely locked and for the first time she used the bolt. She then wearily made her way up the stairs to her bed for some needed sleep.

***

Jenny's parents arrived a week later, having phoned the SSAFA sister every day to check on their daughter. They were aware that she was helping Jenny and she had agreed that they could phone her. Amy, although a bit shy at first, hugged her grandparents then stayed close by their side chatting nonstop. Jenny told them how pleased and relieved she was to see them and when they were seated, went into the kitchen to make some tea.

"Now then my crazy girl, how are you feeling now? Mind, I'll not stand for your nonsense about being ok." Her father had followed her to the kitchen and was eager to check on his daughter.

"I am all the better for seeing you and mum and knowing I'll soon be away from here; I really am much more relaxed. It has been a difficult week. My nerves have been on edge every day afraid Roy might turn up to confront me." Jenny hugged her dad and her relief showed when she began to softly cry.

"There is no need for any tears, things are going to work out and we will keep you and the children safe from now on."

"I know but it has been so upsetting and I never wanted to part from Roy, but I just cannot take any more of his behaviour…, Dad he is not the same person I married!"

Amy interrupted them and demanded to know when the tea was coming, "Grandma said she is parched and sent me to hurry you up."

Jenny and her dad both laughed. "Just coming, tell grandma it won't be two ticks." Jenny carried on making the tea and her dad followed Amy back to his wife.

Later in the evening, the children now in bed asleep, Jenny and her parents could discuss Roy and his behaviour and all agreed that Jenny leaving him here was the best action to take. They were sympathetic to Jenny's feelings and expressed how sorry they were for the situation she has found herself in. Her dad told Jenny she did not have to worry anymore, everything was taken care of and she would be flying home with them in a few days.

"My only worry now is that the children will miss Roy. Charlie not as much as Amy, he is still very young, but Amy has already been asking me where her daddy is and has she done something bad that he hasn't come home."

"You could tell them he is going on an exercise and that is why they won't see him for a while. Also, they are going on a holiday to grandma and grandads. Best not to tell them anymore just yet."

"Do you think this separation will become final Jenny?" Her mum had a worried look.

"I don't know yet. Roy would need to completely stop drinking alcohol because that seems to be what drives him to act badly. I can't trust him and I feel that even if we did get back together, I would be anxious he might be abusive again." Jenny became very thoughtful and her dad changed the subject.

"We will take Amy and Charlie on some days out so they can enjoy themselves. You will be more relaxed when we get you back home with us. You will be in a better frame of mind to think about your future then."

Everything was going to plan. Jenny, with help from mum and dad, had packed up their belongings in the wooden crates that the SSAFA sister had arranged for her. Her clothes and the children's clothes were packed into two suitcases and then a separate bag with some toys and drinks for the journey back to England. She was already feeling less anxious and could not wait to get on the plane.

This mood was ruined when on the day they were to leave, there was a visit from Roy. He arrived accompanied by two military police and the SSAFA sister who was full of apologies, but told Jenny Roy wanted to see her and the children before they all went back to England.

Roy looked very sad and Jenny almost felt sorry for him. Amy was so excited to see her daddy and when she asked him when he was going away on exercise, Roy looked puzzled and glanced at Jenny. After telling his daughter that he hoped that he wouldn't be away too long, Amy seemed pleased and reluctantly was led away by her granny. Roy asked Jenny to step outside so that they could talk.

"It's too late to try and change my mind. I am leaving here this afternoon and you are the one to blame." Jenny was not going to let Roy tell her he wouldn't do it again or say sorry which was not enough now.

"I know Jenny and you have every right to be angry at me, but this time I promise you that I will change. You and the children are my world and I know I don't deserve you, but please don't make this final, please I'm begging you. Have a holiday with your parents and then come back to me. Please I beg you, I will change, I promise."

"I warned you what would happen if you hit me again and now, I don't trust you to change. I need this separation from you so I can think about our future. You like being in the army, so make the most of this. You can visit the children when you have leave but I'm telling you in advance you cannot stay with me if you do visit."

"I can see you are still angry with me and are not going to change your mind so all I can do is let you go and hope there could be a future for us. I will miss you; Amy and Charlie and I would really like to visit just as soon as I can."

With that he hugged both children telling them to be good for mummy and after a brief goodbye to Jenny, he turned and left with the two policemen following behind.

The SSAFA sister wished Jenny lots of luck and asked her if she would write to let her know how they were getting on. Jenny promised she would and thanked her for all the help, then with a brief hug the sister went on her way waving at the children as she went.

CHAPTER 12

At last, the plane was landing on English soil and Jenny gave a big sigh of relief knowing she could at last be safe from Roy. Her parents had kept the children amused on the flight home so Jenny could relax and sleep if she wanted to. They made their way to the car park where her dad's new car was parked. The rest of the journey to her parents' home appeared to go by quickly and the familiar scenery cheered up Jenny.

It took a few days to get used to a different routine, but Jenny found having her mum there to help with the children was ideal. Amy loved to play in the large garden and her grandad was letting her help to plant vegetables. He had given her an area where she could plant some flower seeds and was teaching her how to care for them as they grew.

While Jenny had been away, she had from time-to-time written letters to her old friend Mary. Jenny was so happy to hear the news from Mary that the fertility treatment had finally worked and Mary had gotten pregnant and had a baby. Little Martin was now six months old and Jenny was planning a trip to visit her and at last meet Martin.

It was now two weeks since arriving at her parents' home and today, Jenny was on her way to Mary's house. That was another change Jenny couldn't wait to see, Mary and her husband had been given a house on a new housing estate and had been living there for four months now. Mary had yet to meet Charlie who had been born in Germany and so arriving at the house was chaotic for the first half hour with Mary wanting to hold Charlie and Jenny getting to know Martin. When all the greetings were over, there was lots of chat over a cup of tea while Amy kept the two boys occupied playing with the toys.

"It's so good to see you again Jenny. I am so sorry it has to be under such circumstances."

"Well, it's great to see you again also and to meet your longed-for baby."

"Yes, he was definitely wanted and he is such a good baby. John is so happy and helps with his feeds and everything. He is a natural and after waiting all these years we both have our little family at last." Mary was smiling the whole time and happiness shone from her eyes.

"You got lucky with this house as well, it is lovely and with a garden also for Martin to play in when he is older."

"After you left to go to Germany, we all got a letter telling us that we would be rehoused to council houses because all the old terraced ones were to be demolished. It was a bit of a shock I can tell you but when we were finally given the keys to this house, we couldn't believe our eyes. A brand-new house with all the mod cons, inside toilet, bathroom and a lovely kitchen with hot running water. We were so happy to have a new baby and a new house all within months of each other."

Jenny also felt happiness for Mary and John but couldn't help a slight feeling of sadness. She had wanted to visit the street where she used to live and show Amy the house where she had been born. On telling Mary this, she told Jenny it was all gone, flattened to the ground and that it hadn't taken them long to demolish them just as soon as everyone was rehoused.

It had been a lovely afternoon visiting her old friend and it was agreed that Jenny would visit the following week. On her way back to her parents' home, Jenny met someone she went to school with. He had been in the same class as Jenny, but they had not been close friends because he had hung out with a group of lads and Jenny with her mates. Nevertheless, when he saw Jenny approaching in the opposite direction, he stopped her immediately to say hello.

Jenny was startled at first but on recognising who it was she smiled and said "Jamie Johnson, fancy seeing you after all these years. How are you doing, married I presume?"

"Yes, it's been quite some years since we sat in the same classroom. I was married, didn't work out though so have been a free man for a year. How are you, obviously married and two lovely little ones I see?"

"Do you live in the area?" Jenny asked, "I seem to remember you lived on the other side of the river."

"Yes, I live a few doors from your parents' house. I helped your dad dig his garden a few months ago. We have become quite friendly. Ted is a nice chap and we get on well despite our different ages."

"Oh, I see. Dad hasn't mentioned you, although he wouldn't because I have been away in Germany." Jenny was wondering if Jamie was so friendly with her dad, whether they had discussed her and the troubles she was having. She needn't have worried though.

"Yes, your dad did tell me you were over there, husband in the army I believe he said. Are you having a visit with your parents? How long will you be here for?" Jamie suddenly stopped talking, "Sorry I sound really nosy. I don't mean to be."

"That's ok. It's nice to meet someone from my past. I am staying with my parents for now, marriage not working out but that is a long story," she whispered so Amy couldn't hear that."

"Sorry to hear that and you with children. It must be difficult having to cope on your own."

"Well, I have my parents for now and they help me a lot with the children. I am sure they love having them around."

"That's good and you'll probably see me again soon as your dad needs some help with repairing his shed roof. So, I had better let you get off home. It looks like your little girl is getting bored with my chat." He laughed and ruffled Amy's hair.

"Yes, I had better get them home for their tea. It has been very nice chatting with you and I will probably see you when you come to help my dad."

With that last remark, they said their goodbyes and Jenny hurried on towards home. She couldn't help herself thinking over the meeting with Jamie and what a nice man he seemed to have turned into.

***

After meeting Jamie Johnson, it was another two weeks when they met again. Just as he had told her, he came round to help her dad. Jenny had spoken about him to her dad, who told her that Jamie was a nice lad, very polite and helpful and he liked him a lot.

Being mostly busy with the garden shed, Jenny did not see much of Jamie. She was also kept busy writing a letter to Roy in answer to the one she had received the week before asking if she and the children were settled in with her parents. Jenny felt it was only right that she kept him informed, especially about the children.

Later that afternoon her dad, accompanied by Jamie, came inside to have a tea break. During this time, Amy kept Jamie busy showing him her various toys and telling him the names of her many teddies. Jenny apologised to Jamie for being pestered by her daughter, but he smiled and said it was alright and that he loved children. He sat Charlie on his knee who chuckled away every time Jamie tickled him.

"Do you have any of your own? Jenny was curious rather than being nosey.

"No, my wife did not want children and this caused problems between us."

"Was that the reason you are getting divorced?" Jenny blushed realising that she was now sounding nosy.

"Not really, although it didn't help because I wanted to have children. Amanda, my wife, went off with another man, a friend of mine actually. So, that ended our marriage for good."

"I am so sorry to hear that. It's not surprising you're getting divorced."

"What about you, will you be returning to Germany and your husband?"

Jenny was quiet for some time occupied with her thoughts before she replied. "I'm not quite sure yet. I still have mixed feelings because I never wanted my marriage to be so full of problems, but I am slowly coming to terms with what happened and now know I will have a big decision to make about our future."

"It's early days for you, but me, I have realised by now that my marriage has ended. The solicitor is dealing with the progression of the divorce which could take months to finalise." Jamie looked sad and it seemed like he might cry. Then to her surprise he told her that he knew about her problems she had been having with Roy. "Your dad mentioned to me a while ago that he was worried about you believing your husband may have an issue with drink and his temper."

"Oh, I see! My dad is not very good at keeping

secrets, but then if he was worrying about me, it was good he found someone to talk to."

"Well, I am a good listener. If you ever feel the need to talk then I am your man. I know in these situations it is difficult to talk to parents for fear of worrying them. You hardly know me, but I hope you can see me as a good friend?" Jamie smiled and looked slightly embarrassed.

"I could certainly use a good friend, especially one who has also had a troubled marriage and will surely understand."

Jenny's dad was eager to get back to the shed. He didn't want to keep Jamie and his help longer than was necessary. With a wave to Amy and a quick "see you soon," to Jenny, Jamie followed her dad out to the garden. Jenny had mixed feelings over their conversation but one thing she did know was that she really liked Jamie and chatting to him had stirred feelings she hadn't felt for some time.

CHAPTER 13

It was several weeks before she saw Jamie again. He popped round to see if Jenny and the children would like to go with him to the fair which was in town just for the week. Without hesitation, Jenny agreed to go saying she was intending to take the children to the fair anyway, but it would be nice to have Jamie accompanying them. Her parents thought it was a great idea and commented on how they thought it was most kind of Jamie to offer to go with Jenny. Her mum, who declined to join them, commented that it was much better to have help with the children than to try managing on her own.

It had been arranged to go Wednesday afternoon when the school children would be at school so it would be much quieter and with no waiting to get on the rides. Amy and Charlie squealed with delight on the small roundabouts and enjoyed the ice cream Jamie bought for them, although Charlie got most of it on his face and down his coat. All in all, a good time was had by all and back at home Jenny thanked Jamie for such a lovely day.

"I enjoyed it too, especially seeing the children enjoying themselves. It was a nice treat for me. Maybe we can have another day out somewhere, that is, unless you'd rather not?"

Jenny blushed slightly but smiled saying, "That would be nice. The children don't get out much and you were a good help with them at the fair which they appeared to enjoy a lot."

"That's settled then, we shall go for a walk and visit the park. There is a small café there and we could have tea and cake. I'm sure Amy and Charlie would like that. What do you say, would that be a good idea? As friends of course. I have one more week of my holiday from work so what d'you say we go on Monday?"

"Yes, I would like that and I know the children would too. So, Monday it is, that's a date." Jenny gave a little laugh, "Well not exactly a date. Just two friends out enjoying a walk."

Jamie laughed too, "Exactly! The very idea we could be dating. Don't worry I will act in a proper manner. No hand holding or that sort of thing. Wouldn't want to give others anything to question our relationship." Jenny felt embarrassed. What did it matter what anyone who happened to see them together thought? With that Jenny thanked Jamie once more and said goodbye saying she would see him Monday afternoon unless it was raining.

Later that evening Jenny silently contemplated the day she had just had with Jamie. Her thoughts were all over the place. Could this just be a normal friendship, or could it develop into something more? Jenny couldn't decide which she would like it to be. She really liked being in Jamie's company.

He was kind and gentle especially with Amy and Charlie; the sort of man she wished she had married in the first place. The last thought confused her, she was a married woman, separated from her husband and with her future with him yet to be decided.

Suddenly, Jenny felt the tears trickling down her cheeks. She hadn't cried much since leaving Roy but now, all these confusing thoughts had brought on a deep sadness. In her head she was sure she knew what she had to do, but her heart appeared to be resisting. Did she still love Roy? She wasn't quite sure of her feelings for him in that way. Was she prepared to live a life of anxiety with his behaviour? No, she was sure of that. How could she live a life always protecting herself and her children? Even if Roy assured her that he had changed and would never be violent to her again, how could she trust him? He certainly didn't resemble the man she fell in love with and although there would always be a bond between them, being the father of her children, it was now becoming clearer in her mind what she must do. It really didn't matter where her friendship with Jamie might lead to, she now realised that she would not be returning to Roy. She now knew her life could be a happier one.

****

Monday came and Jenny felt a twinge of excitement at the thought of going out again with Jamie. Getting the children ready to go out on their walk, Jenny's mum cautioned her daughter to take things slowly and enjoy being a friend to Jamie. This had occurred because the day before, Jenny had told her parents of her decision to stay separated from Roy and so ending any hope of reconciliation with him.

Jenny's parents were sad but in agreement that this would be for the best not only for Jenny, but Amy and Charlie deserved to grow up in a happy home. They were also pleased that she was going out for a walk with Jamie, but her dad warned her to be careful because being on the rebound from a bad marriage could lead to mistakes being made for the future. Jenny had assured her dad that she was in control of her feelings and that Jamie and herself were just good friends both with broken marriages, so they understood each other.

Jamie arrived with a beaming smile and playfully ruffled Charlie's hair. "Shall we get off then? The sun is shining, and the park awaits two excited children."

"I'll just grab my handbag and then I am ready."

While Jenny went off to find her bag, Jamie turned his attention to her dad, "Hiya Ted, how's things with you? Have you any more jobs you want my help with? You only have to ask, you know."

Although Jenny's dad liked this young man a lot, he could not help himself but warned Jamie of Jenny's delicate state of mind, "I don't need any help just yet. Thanks for asking. I just want to ask a favour of you though."

"Ask away Ted, you know I'm always willing to help you in any way I can."

"Well, it's about Jenny. I'm concerned for her state of mind at the moment. You know her circumstances and I don't want her to have any more trauma to deal with. So, I was wondering where this friendship of yours might be leading to. I'm not interfering, don't think that, but I do worry about my daughter's happiness you see."

Jamie was taken aback just for a moment, but he could see Jenny's dad only had her interests at heart. "You have no need to worry, we are just good friends and I believe Jenny knows this and is happy about it. I must confess that I like her very much and I would never hurt her. I would be enormously happy if our friendship developed into something more, but I realise Jenny has a lot to sort out, especially her feelings concerning her husband and their future. So, I am just happy to be her friend and a shoulder to lean on if she wants that, and if she returns to Germany then I will miss her but will be happy for her."

Jenny's dad was happy with what Jamie said and

now felt he could trust him to be thoughtful and tread carefully with her. He decided not to mention that Jenny had come to a decision about her future with Roy. He felt that was for Jenny to say if she wanted Jamie to know.

The two friends set off with the children and made their way to the country park which was about half an hour away. There weren't many people around as they walked along the pathway. Not that they would have noticed as they chatted constantly. Jenny had realised she didn't know what kind of job Jamie had and so she was curious to find out.

"Where exactly do you work? I've never asked before and dad hasn't mentioned it."

"I am a civil engineer and work on drafting drawings for potential buildings to be built."

"That sounds interesting. Do you actually draw the plans for new buildings, like an Architect?"

"Oh no, I'm not an Architect, they design the building. I am more of a draughtsman who follows the instructions of what is wanted and draws the shape and measurements of rooms etc."

"Well, it must be a very rewarding job and I bet you're good at it."

"I did study at university and have always had an interest in how buildings are built and when I found this job advertised, I applied and got accepted. I've been with Palmer & Sons for five years now and wouldn't want to work anywhere else."

"Sounds like you're settled there and happy in your work."

"I certainly am, and the wages are good, so what's not to like!"

"Before I got married, I was a secretary in a factory where sports equipment was produced. I was always running errands for my boss between the different departments. Sometimes I felt like a slave to him, but my colleagues were great, so it wasn't too bad really."

"So, you can type? That must have needed some training. I wouldn't know one end of a typewriter to another."

"Yes, I ended up with quite a fast speed on the typewriter, but now I would probably be all fingers and thumbs. It's a skill for which I trained at secretarial college, but if you don't use it, you lose it, so the saying goes."

"I'm sure you could get your speed back in no time at all if you went back to work that is. But I expect with the two little ones here and your future not decided, getting a job would be the last thing on your mind."

"I might have to consider doing just that. Mum has said she would willingly look after Charlie and Amy if I wanted to go out to work. I need to give it some serious thought because I can't go on living free with my parents for the future."

"Oh, so you have made your mind up. Does this mean you are not intending to go back to Germany after all?"

"Well, I have been giving my future some serious thought and although I have only just recently decided, the answer to your question is yes, I'm thinking of a permanent separation from my husband. My future with him would be very precarious and I don't want me and the children to live like that. So, yes there you are, at last I've made my mind up about my future. I just need to sort out if I should go on living with my parent's or renting my own place? Either way I would need to work to pay my way."

"Well, although it really is none of my business, I feel sure you're doing the right thing. If you were to go back to Roy, you and the children could end up seriously hurt if he hasn't changed his behaviour. I could never be violent towards a woman and don't understand what drives a man to do that."

"Nor me! I only wish I could know the answer to that myself. When we married, he was kind and loving although he was somewhat childish and liked to play tricks on people. One evening he played a trick on me, scared me half to death pretending to be someone trying to break into our home."

"That sounds horrible. Why would he do that to you and what did you say to him?"

"At the time I didn't say much, I called a neighbour for help, and he called the police. They were quite annoyed with Roy and one of them gave him a serious talking to. I know Roy felt humiliated about that, he told me so one time when he was being violent to me."

"He must be holding a grudge about it but that shouldn't give him an excuse to be abusive to you."

"I don't know, although his manner towards me did change after that. Maybe it's my fault he is angry and violent, though it only happens when he's been drinking. Perhaps I was too hasty in running to that neighbour for help."

"Now, don't, don't you do that to yourself! Blaming yourself for his behaviour. It's not your fault, that I am certain of. What sort of husband tries to frighten his wife by playing a practical joke like he did? More like he has a split personality and can be nice most of the time but then nasty when the drink gives him courage to be."

"Anyway, it is in the past now and my decision to leave has put an end to him being violent to me again. So, let's change the subject to more pleasant things. Anyway, we have reached the swings and playground so let's give the children some fun."

Jamie helped Charlie out of his pushchair and the toddler immediately headed for the swings. Jamie guided him to the baby swing and strapped him onto the swing. Charlie squealed every time Jamie pushed the swing. He was certainly enjoying it. Jamie's thoughts turned to what Jenny had just told him. If her husband could be violent after drinking alcohol, then could she really be safe away from him. He is not going to take kindly to being told Jenny is not returning to him and although being in Germany didn't matter, it's only a plane ride away and he could get leave from the army. Jamie's thoughts troubled him. Was he being silly, or could Jenny be yet to face more danger from her husband? He decided that just in case he would be on the alert for any trouble that should occur.

After the children played for a while in the playground, they all headed to the small café and sat down to enjoy tea and cake. Amy was delighted with her cake and munched merrily away, while Charlie was too tired to eat and promptly fell asleep on Jenny's lap who seemed quiet and withdrawn and Jamie wondered if she wasn't enjoying the afternoon out.

He didn't need to worry though, on the journey homeward she told him she had really enjoyed herself and thanked Jamie for such a lovely afternoon. Also telling him it had been good to talk to someone she felt understood just how she was feeling. Jamie was pleased that Jenny and the children had a good time with him again, but he now couldn't get the anxious feeling that Jenny may yet be in danger. With this thought came the realisation that he cared very much about her and not just as a friend. Could he be falling in love with her?

CHAPTER 14

Over the next few weeks, life for Jenny was a mix of helping her mum cook and clean, going on walks sometimes with Jamie and sometimes alone to gather her thoughts when certain things were constantly on her mind. Like receiving a letter from Roy which stated he had some leave due and was planning to come to England and visit her and the children. Jenny had been filled with all manner of emotions at this news and was dreading Roy's visit, if only because she was planning to tell him of her decision not to go back to Germany and that she was planning to seek a divorce. Jenny has already got an appointment with a solicitor to set things in motion for a divorce on the grounds of physical and mental abuse being the cause of a breakdown in the marriage with no reconciliation possible.

Roy had given her a date of his visit which was

now fast approaching and the nearer she got to the date the more anxious she became. On telling her parents of the visit and how she was feeling, they too were a little worried and suggested that she should not see him alone. Her dad had offered to stay with her while her mum remained close by in another room if she wanted them to. Jenny had told them that sounded like a good idea and so it was agreed this should be the best for her safety, although Jenny told them she did not expect Roy to be violent to her with the children around and they would be there to see their daddy again.

Jamie was also worried when Jenny informed him of the expected visit. He said he hoped the visit would be at the weekend so he could be there for her if there was any trouble. He even suggested if it were on a workday then he would take the day off just in case she might need his help. Jenny assured him that his help would be appreciated but she told him that she didn't want any altercations with Roy which could result in some harm. In fact, she asked him if he would please keep his distance so as not to give Roy any ideas that there was anything going on with her and Jamie. He answered this by telling her that he cared for her very much and wanted to support her but promised he would stay away if that was what she wanted but he made Jenny promise that she would send word to him if there was any danger of Roy becoming abusive.

It was Saturday and the day of the visit. Jenny prepared Amy and Charlie by informing them that their daddy was coming to spend some time with them. She also asked Amy not to mention Jamie to her daddy and to keep it their secret for now. Amy agreed she would not mention him but asked that if Jamie were just a friend why would her daddy be cross. After Jenny explained that Roy might be upset to hear that they had all been going for walks and to the park sometimes when he wasn't able to do that being so far away, Amy nodded and stated that she understood and it would be a good idea to keep it a secret.

Roy arrived later that morning with flowers for Jenny and presents for the children in hand and there was much excitement from the children who were so pleased to see him again. After greeting her parents, Betty suggested she go into the kitchen to prepare some lunch.

"Will you be staying for lunch?" her mum asked Roy.

"Oh, I don't want you to go to any trouble,

perhaps Jenny and the children would like to go out to a restaurant with me."

Taking Jenny by surprise she quickly replied, "That would be lovely, but we were planning on having a family lunch all together, here at home."

Roy looked disappointed but then cheerily said, "Yes, that would be nice. I realise springing that on you wasn't the best thing to do so maybe I can arrange for us to have a meal out on another day while I'm on leave."

"How long is your leave and where are you staying?" Jenny was eager to know his plans.

"I have three weeks to stay in England and I'm staying at my mums for now. I remembered you told me I would not be welcome to stay with you." He said in a direct manner.

Jenny noticed a slight grievance in his voice but was determined not to let this bother her or feel guilty. "Is your mother well? It seems a long time since we last met?"

"She has a lot of pain from her Arthritis but is still managing to work, though she is going to retire early so only has one more year at work. Of course, she is thrilled to have me visiting her but misses not seeing Amy and Charlie. It has been a long time since there has been any contact with them."

Now Jenny was feeling guilty, this was certainly true, and she made a mental note to make time to take the children to visit. Jenny had decided that she should wait to tell Roy about the divorce. If he were going to be around for three weeks, then it would be best to wait until nearer the end of the last week to tell him. She felt certain he would not be happy about the divorce, and this might cause some trouble between them.

***

The next two weeks there were many more visits from Roy. He even took the children to see his mother, after all she was their granny who hadn't seen them in a while. This eased Jenny's guilt but she still planned to visit his mum more often. Roy was always on his best behaviour when he visited and with the weather being warm, he often played football or a chase game in the garden with the children while Jenny sat close by keeping an eye on things. He also took them to the park twice and as he appeared to be behaving like a father should, Jenny agreed to go with him mainly because she felt she could trust him to behave. On such outings, there was never any talk about their circumstances, so these were quite enjoyable.

Amy kept to her agreement to keep the secret and Jamie had not been mentioned. However, he did come round on several of Roy's visits, being introduced as Ted's friend and helper. Jenny's dad would spend time with Jamie out in the garden shed and update him on the situation regarding Roy. The children were too busy with Roy to pay Jamie much attention, so everything was going well so far.

The last week of Roy's leave arrived and he asked Jenny to go with him on Tuesday evening for a meal at the restaurant, saying it was because he didn't know just when he might get leave again and he wanted to share some time alone with her. Jenny was hesitant to agree then suggested she would speak to her parents as she needed them to babysit.

Her parents were anxious about Jenny being alone with him but felt better after Jenny assured them that Roy couldn't do anything in a restaurant and she would order a taxi home soon after the meal was over. So she told Roy it was ok to go for a meal with him and he arranged it for the following evening.

They went to an Italian restaurant in the centre of town and Jenny, although nervous, couldn't help being a little excited. It had been a long time since she had been out for a meal and found herself quite looking forward to it. During the meal Jenny felt a sadness creep over her as this would be the last time she ever went out with her husband, made worse by the fact Roy didn't know this.

Telling him about the divorce was yet to come and because he was leaving in two more days, she knew it would have to be the next day when she told him their marriage would be ending. Their conversation was mainly about Amy and Charlie, Roy stating how much they had grown, and that Amy was a right little chatterbox. Roy said he was going to miss them and then out of the blue he asked Jenny to return with him to Germany.

"Please Jenny give me another chance, I am so sorry for how I treated you and I promise that will never happen again. I have missed you so much and if it weren't for being in the army and kept busy, I think I would go mad."

Jenny was thoughtful. Was she perhaps wrong? Could Roy have changed and had he learned a lesson from their separation? She had changed though; she wasn't going to let him play on her emotions. "If I were to return and later in time you mistreated me again, you would have betrayed my trust for the second time, and I am not sure I can trust you to keep your word." She couldn't look at him fearing she might crumble and give in.

"Please…, please Jenny, you can trust me, I don't know what got into me, but the army has shown me that being angry and fighting is for certain occasions when against an enemy. I can assure you Jenny that you're not my enemy, you are my wife and I love you."

"I don't know what to say right now, you have sprung this on me, and my feelings are in a muddle. I think it's best if I sleep on what you are asking and give you my answer tomorrow." She bowed her head knowing what her answer would be the next day. She had already made her mind up that this would be the end of her marriage and she was not going to let Roy saying sorry again change her mind. She couldn't allow herself to start feeling sorry for him. She must think of her safety and the children's safety. It would be her fault if she gave in to him now, after all he was probably feeling sorry for himself, and the good behaviour probably wouldn't last for long.

Getting into the taxi to go home, Roy pulled her to him and gently kissed her on the lips. "I hope you have enjoyed your evening with me and that your answer tomorrow will be the one I want it to be."

Jenny quickly got inside the taxi and sat tense in the seat. As it pulled away Roy waved and blew her a kiss. This was too much for Jenny and the tears flowed freely and silently until reaching her parents' home. Roy had been like the man she married throughout the evening but still she had many doubts, how could she forget the violent behaviour and how frightened and helpless she felt? She couldn't under any circumstance let her heart rule her head. But she was sad that the divorce would break Amy's heart, Charlie was too young to realise what that meant.

Seeing the children with their daddy these past weeks has shown her just how much Amy loves him, but she will have to be happy with visits from him in the future. No matter that Jenny felt sorry for hurting

Roy, it was the right thing to do to protect them just in case Roy hadn't or couldn't change his behaviour.

***

The next morning Jenny was up very early. She had tossed and turned most of the night worrying about how Roy would take the news that their marriage was about to end.

Her mum gave her a big hug and tried to reassure her that this was the right thing to be doing and Jenny's dad took her hand, looked directly into her eyes, and told her that he would always be there for her, and the children and she must be steadfast in her decision no matter how heart-breaking it must be for her.

Amy as usual talked non stop about what she would do when her daddy arrived later that morning. Not once during the past three weeks had she asked her mummy why daddy was not staying with them in grandad's house. Maybe she knew that this would be how it was going to be, at least believing daddy lived in Germany and they were staying with her grandma and grandad. Whatever her young mind had decided, it appeared to Jenny that her daughter was happy. She asked herself how Amy would be after today when saying goodbye to Roy? They were all going to the park and then the local cafe for lunch before returning to the house for Roy to play in the garden with the children for the last time. The next day he would be gone again.

The day had gone well so far, her parents had been polite to Roy but not over friendly. The children had enjoyed ice cream after fish and chips for lunch and were now back home in the garden kicking a ball around with Roy. Jenny had decided that it might be better to get Roy on his own and tell him her decision about the future of their marriage. So after an hour of play, her mum came into the garden and suggested the children go into the house for some milk and biscuits while mummy and daddy had a chat. Reluctantly the children agreed, much to the relief of Jenny.

"I am glad we can have some time on our own," Roy looked expectantly at Jenny and pulled her down to sit next to him on the garden bench.

Trembling slightly Jenny looked away from him and began to speak, "I realise you are hoping for a good outcome to the request you made last evening, and I have come to a decision about our future together."

"Please oh please let it be a positive answer. I could hardly sleep last night for thinking it might be over between us."

She stared straight ahead as she spoke her next words, "I am sorry Roy, but my decision is that I cannot return with you and in fact I have been in contact with a solicitor to start divorce proceedings."

Roy sat silent for what seemed like ages as though he was trying to process what she had just told him. He then spoke again, softly at first but then in a raised voice, "You already knew this last night didn't you and you let me sit there and make a fool of myself. Giving me hope that things between us might be ok after all?"

"Yes, I did know that I had decided to end our marriage, but if it is any consolation, I was nearly swayed by your manner towards me these past few weeks. However, I finally came to the decision that I have lost the trust I had for you, I loved the man I married, not the monster who abused me and I am fearful that sometime in the future you might become that person again."

"I promise I won't be him again. I love you and have missed you and you can trust me. Please don't go through with this divorce, I am begging you." Roy appeared distraught at Jenny's revelations.

"It's no use; I have struggled for weeks trying to decide the future not just for me but the children also and eventually I decided I need to keep us safe and secure knowing we can't be hurt ever again."

The mention of the children seemed to make Roy angry, "I would never hurt the children! You must know that, and I have told you time and again that I am sorry for hurting you, but I can see that it is hopeless to try to persuade you that I have changed." Roy suddenly jumped to his feet and grabbing Jenny with both arms, he pulled her violently to her feet and then began shaking her, "You can't do this to me! I won't let you take my children away from me, I love them and if you go through with this divorce, I'll fight you tooth and nail to get custody of them."

Before either could speak again, Jamie was rushing towards them and shouted at Roy to let go of Jenny. He had been watching from the window and when he saw Roy angrily shaking Jenny he just had to intervene. Roy swung around to see who was shouting and when he saw Jamie, he stared angrily at Jenny's face. "Oh, I see! This is why you want a divorce is it?

Here is a lover you have been hiding. It didn't take you long to shower your affections on some other bloke!"

He spat the words at Jenny's face and his grip tightened. "Well let's see just how much he means to you shall we?" With that he swung around and lunged at Jamie lashing out with his fists. Jamie fought back and managed to land some good punches and knock Roy to the ground. Jenny rushed to get between them shouting for them to stop fighting and as Roy got to his feet, she tried to pacify him.

"You're being stupid; Jamie is dad's friend and not my lover, so you have got things wrong, and he is not the reason for my decision. You have just shown me that you can't be trusted, and you still have a temper. You are the reason for my decision and must own up to your behaviour and causing the breakdown of our marriage." Jenny angrily shouted these words at Roy, finally standing up to him. "I would like you to leave now. I've nothing more to say except that you will be hearing from my solicitor."

Roy appeared to come to his senses and glared at Jamie. He wasn't sure that he believed Jenny but not wanting anymore trouble he grudgingly walked past them saying as he went, "I will say goodbye to my children and don't try to stop me. At least they don't see me as a monster." Instinctively Jenny rushed forward to protect the children but was stopped in her tracks by her dad.

"Leave it Jenny, your mum is in the house with the children, and she will not let him harm them. Anyway, at least let him do this, after all, his world has just come crashing down and deep down, he must surely be upset at not going to be a family anymore. So, let him have these last few minutes with Amy and Charlie. It will be a while before he sees them again and as a father myself, I know that must hurt him."

They all stood and watched him go but Jenny couldn't help wondering if he meant what he said, and she would have a fight on her hands.

CHAPTER 15

A month had gone by when Jenny's solicitor wrote to her with a request that she visit his office. Leaving the children in the care of their granny, Jenny was nervous as she stood outside the solicitor's door. Giles and Benson had been practising as solicitor's for over ten years and had a very good reputation in the town. Jenny was there to see Mr Benson, the older of the two partners. She had never needed a solicitor before and was unsure of the proceedings for obtaining a divorce. However, she had every faith that Mr Benson would explain everything.

Knocking hard on the door, a voice called out that she should enter. As she did so, Mr Benson came around his huge desk to greet her. "Good morning, Mrs Crabtree. I'm so pleased you could come this morning. Please take a seat. Can I offer you some tea, or coffee if you prefer?"

Jenny sat on the edge of the seat on the other side of the desk, "Thank you but I don't want any tea but perhaps I could have a glass of water. My mouth is very dry."

Realising she must be nervous, hence the dry mouth, the solicitor poured Jenny some water and placed it on the desk in front of her. "There now, please don't be nervous. I assure you, I don't bite." He gave a little chuckle at his joke. "I have asked you to visit me today to have a chat and sort out some of the preliminary proceedings to start the process of your desire for a divorce from Mr Crabtree. Now let us get down to finding out what your reasons are for wanting a divorce."

Jenny took a drink of water to enable her to speak. "Yes, that is correct. I want a divorce because my husband was being violent to me, and I couldn't take anymore."

"Oh, yes, I see from your initial contact that you have been married for approximately five years and you have two children, a boy and a girl and your husband is serving in the British army living in Germany at this time. Is this correct?"

Yes, that's right and I went to Germany to live there with him but after our son was born his behaviour changed and he began drinking a lot which appeared to make him violent. There were several occasions when he was violent towards me and so I left him to come back to stay with my parents in England."

"Was he ever violent to the children?" The solicitor showed he was listening.

"No, never. It was always directed at me, but I would stay in my children's bedroom to protect them, but he never followed me there."

Mr Benson was writing down all that Jenny was telling him. He put down his pen and there was silence between them for several seconds. Then he spoke again, "Hmm, when did you actually leave your husband in Germany?"

I have been at my parents' home for almost a year now. My husband came once to visit for three weeks, but didn't stay with me, instead he stayed at his mother's house. He would come almost daily to play with the children or take them out somewhere."

"I see, and how was his behaviour towards you? Did you have any violent episodes from him?"

Jenny hung her head down. Should she tell him about Roy's Behaviour on his last day visiting after telling him her decision to end their marriage. She didn't want to put fuel on the fire, but then again Roy's behaviour had shown Jenny that he hadn't changed his ways. So, after clearing her throat she told him, "He was fine until the very last day before he had to return to Germany. I told him I would be making my break from him permanent, and he just lost it. He even attacked my dad's friend Jamie."

"About this Jamie, is it correct that he lives a few doors from your parent's home?

"Yes, that's right. He is a nice person, very helpful to my dad and has been kind to me and the children. I remember him from our school days but we didn't speak to each other. He had his friends and I had mine."

The solicitor was thoughtful and began flipping through some papers in a file. Then on finding the paper he was looking for he spent some minutes reading what was on it. After finishing reading, he looked up at Jenny, a rather questioning look. "Mrs Crabtree, I have to tell you that your husband's solicitor has written to me stating that Mr Crabtree is counteracting your reasons for desiring a divorce."

Jenny was surprised by this and was curious to know what Roy was up to. "What does that mean? Is Roy denying he was violent, and our marriage hadn't broken down? Because I can't trust him and need to keep myself and my children safe."

"Well now, he certainly has come up with a different reason for you wanting a divorce and if true it puts a very different aspect on obtaining a divorce. He is even applying for custody of your two children."

Jenny couldn't speak. She was taken aback that Roy may be lying to his solicitor and denying any violence during their marriage. She took another drink of the water before she was able to speak again. There were yet even more unsuspecting aspects of the lengths Roy was willing to go to get back at Jenny.

"I can see you were not expecting this change of circumstances, but let us work through what he is stating, shall we? The man you say is your father's friend, is he called Jamie Johnson who lives four doors away from your parents?"

Jenny is puzzled why Jamie's name should be mentioned, "Yes, that is his name but why do you ask?"

"Have you ever been out with this Jamie, such as to the park with your children or even to a restaurant for a meal while you have been living at your parents' home?"

Well, yes, I told you he has been very kind and offered to accompany myself and the children to a fair and also the country park. I also went for a meal with him. It was Christmas and he wanted to cheer me up."

"Please be honest with me when I ask my next question to you, "Has there been any romantic involvement with this Jamie?"

"No, of course not! He has just been a very good friend to me and the children. I don't know why you are asking me this or even why you should bring Jamie into this." Jenny was quick to defend herself from this suggestion.

"Mrs Crabtree, I have to inform you that your husband has stated he wants to divorce you because you are romantically involved with Jamie Johnson and have committed adultery. He also states that you are not a fit mother to look after his children, Amy and Charlie."

Jenny could hardly believe what she was hearing and was finding it difficult to speak and deny Roy's accusations. Somehow, she found her voice and when she spoke it was to show her anger she felt for her husband. "How dare he insinuate that. Where is his proof and how did he manage to get the information about Jamie? He only met him once and that was when Roy attacked him because Jamie came to my aid when Roy lashed out at me on that last day of his visit and after I had told him our marriage was over!"

Don't distress yourself Mrs Crabtree. It appears it is only hearsay that your husband thinks he has proof. He does, however, know that you accompanied Jamie to a restaurant for a meal. Would your parents be up to making a statement to support your denial of his accusations?"

"Of course they would be willing. They know nothing romantically has occurred between Jamie and me. As for his suggestion that I am an unfit mother, how can he say that when all I have done is try to protect them from him?"

"He might suggest that they didn't need protecting from him. He could counteract that stating he had never hurt them during your marriage. In fact, he had already stated that his children love him and are happy to spend time with him. Anyway, I can see this has upset you very much and I suggest you go home and digest it all and I will let his solicitor know of your statement and will then be in touch with you again. There is no hurry to sort all this out. I am afraid to tell you that there has to be a two-year separation before you will be granted a divorce. But in the meantime, we can prepare your case to produce at the court."

"Two years separation!" Jenny was alarmed at this piece of news. "That means it will be another year I have to remain separated from Roy. Another year of anxieties worrying if we are safe from him."

"Don't worry, we can apply for a separation order and if necessary, a restraining order if he shows any threatening behaviour towards you. So, go home, inform your parents what we have discussed and try to get on with your life. I will have it all in hand and be in touch soon."

With this he stood up to shake Jenny's hand and wished her a good day. Jenny shook his hand and made her way to the door. Still slightly stunned at the solicitor's revelations. How dare Roy stoop so low as to accuse her of adultery. She felt this situation might be hopeless. How would she prove that what he had told his solicitor wasn't true?

CHAPTER 16

Ted was watching out of the window awaiting Jenny's return. He was eager to know what the solicitor had said. When Jenny finally arrived home, she immediately burst into tears. Ted couldn't understand a word she was saying as she mumbled in between sobs. He did, however, catch the odd word, one of which was adultery. This intrigued him to learn what Jenny was saying. So, sitting her down and facing close to her, he calmed her down until she was speaking normally again.

"Now my darling girl, repeat again what you have just been saying and do it in a calm manner so I can follow what is being said."

Jenny began to speak, slowly and calmly this time, "Roy is counteracting my reasons for getting divorced. He is claiming I have been unfaithful and committed adultery with Jamie."

Ted's mouth was wide open in disbelief. "That's not right, you have never been unfaithful. How can he say that? He doesn't know Jamie, only met him that day when Roy got angry? You and Jamie are just friends, haven't so much as kissed, have you?"

"Of course not and we are just friends. Somehow Roy knew about me going to the park and for walks with Jamie. He even knew I had been to the restaurant for a meal with him last Christmas."

"How could he know all that when he has been in Germany all this time? That's just ridiculous."

"I don't know dad how he found out, but now he believes we are in a relationship and I've probably slept with Jamie. That's why he had told his solicitor these details and so claiming he wants to divorce me because of that." Jenny, head bowed, and face covered by her hands, began to cry again but softly this time and her tears ran slowly down over her hands. She then looked up at her dad and spoke again, "That's not all he had told his solicitor. He also is stating I am a bad mother and he wants custody of the children. Oh dad, what am I going to do? How am I going to prove that it is all lies? He can't get his hands on my children. I will fight him with my last breath if need be." Jenny was now showing some anger and believed with all her heart that her last comment was true.

"Well, all I can say is it shouldn't be up to you to prove that isn't true. It seems to me that Roy should have to show proof of what he is accusing you of. What did you tell the solicitor in answer to that revelation?"

"I told him it wasn't true, and that Jamie was a friend of yours who had been kind to me and the children, but that there was no romance between us."

"Good, so we shall have to question what proof Roy has to prove his accusation and from now on you must be careful not to go anywhere with Jamie."

"The Solicitor told me that I wouldn't be able to get a divorce until I've had two years of separation from Roy. I don't think I want to avoid Jamie for that length of time. It's not fair, his behaviour caused me to leave him and now I am the one being blamed."

"Don't upset yourself sweetheart. I'm sure he can't have any proof. How can he? It just isn't true.

Just being seen out with Jamie does not amount to adultery. So, if you want to go to the park or whatever with him then do it and ignore what Roy thinks he knows. He will need proof and as for him trying to get his hands on the children well…, the SSAFA sister could be a witness to what occurred and also knows he is not a fit father for the children."

Jenny was thoughtful for a while and then spoke again, "You're right dad, Roy has messed up my life enough, so I won't let him prevent me from getting on and enjoying my life from now on. I have a chance of a fresh start away from him, even if I must wait another year. Let him tell all the lies he wants to; I know the truth and like you said so does the SSAFA sister and his Commanding officer for that matter."

"That's my girl. You fight him on this and don't let him get in the way of you living your life. Amy and Charlie want a happy confident mum, not one looking over her shoulder all the time."

"Yes, and I will ignore anything he tells his solicitor and when he comes to visit the children, if he comes that is, I shall not have anything to do with him myself."

Later, when alone, Jenny pondered on her words to her dad. It was one thing saying these things but another to follow them through. Could she be brave enough to ignore Roy's lies or even be confident enough to avoid contact with him from now on? "Damn him, I wish I had never met him." Her next thoughts were more logical, and she reminded herself that had she not met him she wouldn't have two beautiful children in her life. So, she was determined to fight Roy for custody.

***

The day after her visit to the solicitor, Jenny decided to visit Mary. She always felt happy after a chat with her friend. Anyway, it had been several weeks since Mary visited her. It would be little Martin's birthday next week and she wanted to ask Mary what he might like her to buy for him. On the last visit by Mary, she had told Jenny that she was going to have a small gathering for Martin's birthday because being one year old and not yet walking wasn't ideal to have lots of small children around.

On arriving at Mary's house, Jenny found her in the kitchen baking cakes. Jenny offered to help but

Mary insisted she sit down with a cup of tea and tell her all her news since they last got together. Jenny was reluctant to talk about her visit to the solicitor, but Mary was eager to know what had been discussed.

"I'm afraid it's not very good what he told me, but I am determined to fight Roy. I have made up my mind to make sure he doesn't get all his own way."

Jenny's words intrigued Mary and she was even more interested to hear what had been said so she left her baking and sat down opposite her friend to concentrate on what Jenny had to say. "Oh, doesn't sound like it was what you expected to hear, so please tell me so I can understand what happened. You know you can trust me not to pass on what you tell me."

With that Jenny poured her heart out to her friend and Mary didn't say a word until Jenny had told her everything. Even the conversation she had with her dad on returning home from the solicitor.

"Well, that husband of yours has got a cheek. How can he make up such lies and him being miles away and knows nothing? He can't be allowed to get away with accusing you of that when he is the one that abused you. As for having to wait another year before getting divorced, surely that can't be true, can it?"

"It wouldn't be so bad, but I have grown to like Jamie very much. He has been a good friend and the children love being with him, but as for any romance, there has been nothing but friendship between us. I am certainly not letting this stop me from being friends with him."

"Good for you! Don't let Roy beat you down. You're never going back to him, and your life has certainly been better living here away from him, hasn't it?"

"Of course it has, without a doubt, but having to wait another year to be free from him makes me wonder what more to expect from him to cause me trouble?"

"Don't waste another day worrying about him. I feel sure all will be well in the end and if your friendship with Jamie turns into something more, then let it, you deserve someone who will make you and your lovely children happy."

"You're right Mary and I must now concentrate on my life going forward. Starting with me getting a part time job to earn some money. I can't keep taking money off my dad, it's just not fair for my parents to have to support me. So, from tomorrow I will be job hunting, and if you hear of anything suitable, please let me know."

"Of course I will and don't worry anymore, everything will work out for you, just remain positive."

With that last comment from her friend, Jenny prepared to leave, but not before they noticed what Martin was doing. Everything Charlie did, Martin tried to copy him and was crawling after him like his little shadow. This made both women laugh and Mary gave Jenny a friendly hug stating that she was so pleased to be friends with her. Jenny then left with the information about the birthday party and advice that she should buy whatever she wanted for the little boy.

CHAPTER 17

Jenny decided to sign on with an employment agency. She had agreed to do some temping work until she had succeeded in getting her typing skills back up to speed. For this she was going to attend night school on a refresher typing course. Her parents had agreed to look after the children and today Jenny was taking Amy to school perhaps for the last time, then her mum would do this task.

Jamie had taken the news of Roy accusing them of committing adultery very well. In fact, he laughed stating "chance would be a fine thing" to which Jenny had blushed causing Jamie to say sorry and that he meant no offence as this was a serious matter. He did, however, encourage Jenny to remain friends and suggested they still took the children to the park together stating there was no harm in that, to which Jenny was in full agreement.

The employment agency had found Jenny some work in an office doing general clerical work with no typing to do. Although temporary, it was for a long term position as the employee Jenny would be standing in for was going on maternity leave. This was in the office of a large warehouse firm which stored and distributed tools and machinery and was a part time job, working nine in the morning to twelve noon, four days a week. After a week of training by the employee who was going on maternity leave, Jenny would take over the job the following week. The work wasn't difficult except she needed to learn all the different machinery and their part numbers so that when the orders came in on the telephone, she could send this through to the warehouse.

After one month in the job, Jenny had got into a routine and was able to share looking after the children with her mum. She was even able to collect Amy from school and enjoyed the walk with Charlie in his pushchair and chatting at the gates with some of the other mums. Her first pay packet was a very welcome sight and on the Saturday afternoon, accompanied by Jamie, they all went to the toy shop to buy the children a new toy each and then have afternoon tea to celebrate.

***

Jenny's dad drove her to night school every Wednesday and then he came back to collect her. The lessons were proving just to be what she needed to gain her speed in typing. Life was feeling normal again and Jenny had ceased worrying about Roy and his accusations. He hadn't written any letters to her since going back to Germany which slightly annoyed her because she thought he should at least be asking how the children were getting on.

Her dad had stated that it was a good thing not hearing from Roy, only because whenever she had heard from him it was to cause trouble. This perplexed her somewhat and she told her dad this because the children were missing Roy, especially Amy who had been asking when she might see him again. To which her dad had replied that by not seeing him perhaps it was a good thing and Amy would get over missing him. Jenny said she hoped he would be right, but it was a fact that Roy would always be Amy's dad.

***

It was almost as though Jenny had willed it

because the following week, she did receive a letter from Roy. It was a very short matter of fact letter stating he would not be able to visit the children for a few more months because he was going on a three weeks army exercise and then even though he had some leave due he would be going on holiday on a road trip with some army mates. However, he did ask for news of the children.

At first, she felt relieved that there was no nastiness in the letter but then became annoyed that he would go on a holiday with his mates rather than visit the children. "Just typical," she thought, "always putting his own pleasures before his childrens". She decided to let it go and that by the time he did get around to visiting again it would be nearer to getting a divorce and freedom from him.

So, she got on with her life. Throwing herself into work and pleasure time with the children and sometimes with Jamie, but always careful to just remain friends. Her mum was really enjoying looking after the children and her dad was keeping busy making a playhouse for them with some help from Jamie. There were visits from Mary which delighted Jenny and on one such visit she could see Martin taking his first wobbly steps.

The next letter to arrive was an official looking one from Giles and Benson, her solicitor. It was a request that she should visit Mr Benson's office and there was a date and time inserted for the coming week, but should she be unable to visit perhaps a telephone call could be arranged. With the date and time being the following Tuesday afternoon at two o'clock, Jenny would be able to go to their office.

The visit proved very interesting because Mr Benson told Jenny there was news from Roy's solicitor. He had instructed his solicitor to offer Jenny a deal that if she would agree to him having custody of the children, then he would not go ahead with the accusation of adultery. Mr Benson, however, told Jenny not to even consider this and asked her if she had any evidence that would back her accusations of Roy's violent and mental cruelty? In answer to this, Jenny told him about the help she had received from the SSAFA sister in Germany and the meeting with Roy's commanding officer. She then remembered her friend and neighbour in the building where they were living and wondered if she would provide written evidence, even though it had been a while since hearing from her, it would be worth trying this.

Mr Benson also suggested that he didn't think Roy had any evidence of adultery and would not succeed in getting the divorce on these grounds. He then told Jenny that if she had a strong case of physical and violent abuse, Roy would lose the right to get custody of his children as well as helping Jenny get her divorce. He finished their chat by saying he would refuse the deal offered and would request that Roy should provide evidence he had of any adultery. With this he brought the meeting to a close saying he would be in touch again with Jenny just as soon as he had any further news.

Jenny left the solicitor's office and made her way home. Amy and Charlie greeted her with the biggest hugs and kisses which caused Jenny to reinforce her decision that Roy would not win.

She would write to all who might provide evidence and hopefully be able to pass this on to Mr Benson, thereby making her case stronger. That very evening, once the children were in bed, Jenny set about writing letters to the SSAFA sister and Renata. Both letters were quite long by the time she had finished putting all her news into them. She ended them by asking if they could help with writing a letter to her with details supporting the treatment she had received from Roy and any evidence they could report of injuries, such as bruises etc. Sealing the envelopes, Jenny sent a silent prayer that all would be well. She posted them the next day with the hope of receiving the replies she needed.

***

During the next two weeks, Jenny hurried home from work to check if there were any letters for her. On the third week, she received a letter from Renata who had been so pleased to hear from Jenny and to hear how she had been getting on.

With updates from her friend and her children, there was a separate page on which Renata had listed all the occasions she had heard about or seen evidence of Jenny's husband's violent behaviour. At the end of the list, Renata wrote about how she found Jenny's state of anxiety and fear had increased the longer she stayed living with her husband, Roy.

Another two weeks after receiving the letter from Renata, Jenny got a letter from the SSAFA Sister. Not only a letter, but a copy of the report sent to the

Commanding Officer after Jenny had visited the hospital. This was such good evidence that Roy had attacked her and the letter stated her injuries. Jenny was so pleased she had allowed the SSAFA Sister to take her to the hospital.

In the letter from SSAFA were details of her visits to Jenny and explanations of Jenny's state of mind being extremely frightened and anxious about if and when her husband might get drunk and be violent to her again. She also wrote that in her estimation Jenny was a good caring mother and was very protective of the children, especially trying to keep them safely away from her husband whenever he was in a drunken state.

The letter also commented on Jenny's progress since returning to England and was very impressed that Jenny had found herself employment as well as catching up on her typing skill. SSAFA encouraged Jenny to be happy, live her life for herself and the children and lastly, she wished Jenny well in obtaining a divorce and getting custody of Amy and Charlie. The letter cheered Jenny so much that she read it again and again to make sure she had absorbed everything in it.

Her parents read the letters also and were as

pleased as Jenny. They all agreed that these letters were good evidence to help her case for obtaining a divorce. There was just one more thing her dad suggested, "Your mum and I must write a letter stating the change in your mental state since living with us after leaving your husband."

"Would you do that for me? Oh dad, you and mum have been so good to me and have helped me get my life back on track."

Mum now joined in with, "Jenny you're our lovely daughter and it pains me to read those letters and know what you had to endure. Your dad and I would move heaven and earth to see you and the children happy."

"I am happy now mum, thanks to you two but it distresses me knowing I brought my troubles to you. I didn't want you to know what was happening to me because I felt ashamed." With this, Jenny began to cry and her mum rushed forward to hug her daughter. "I never thought Roy could be so cruel, he is not the man I fell in love with and married. They say Love is blind and how right they are, in my case anyway." With this last remark, Jenny dried her eyes and stopped crying.

"You mustn't blame yourself. As far as we are concerned you did nothing wrong, it was Roy who did wrong for behaving as he did. Now he must live with the consequences of his actions, and you shouldn't feel sorry for him." Jenny's dad tried not to show his hate for Roy, but he surely wished he had Roy in front of him so that he could vent his anger at him.

Their conversation was interrupted by Amy followed closely by Charlie. They had both drawn pictures and were eager to show Jenny and their grandparents. Charlie had drawn what resembled a crooked house, but it was Amy's drawing that intrigued the adults.

Her picture showed a house with five stick people outside the house, two which were smaller than the rest. To the side of the picture and away from the house were another two-stick people, one of which appeared to be lying down.

Jenny asked Amy about what she had drawn, and Amy replied, "That is grandad's house," and pointing to the stick people she continued, "This is Granny and Grandad and then mummy with Charlie and me."

"That is very nice and who are the other people in

your picture? They are not standing near us."

Amy appeared to be lost in thought then pointing to the one lying down she said, "That one is daddy and this one is Jamie. He knocked daddy down when they had a fight."

Jenny was taken by surprise at Amy's explanation and she looked towards her parents who both shrugged with a look of amazement. She spoke again to her daughter, "I like your picture very much, but I am puzzled as to why you drew Jamie knocking daddy to the ground. When did you see that happen?"

Amy put her hands on her hips and standing in a bossy manner said to her mummy, "Silly mummy, don't tell me you have forgotten? Daddy got cross at Jamie and hit him and then Jamie hit daddy back and he fell down! That was while daddy was visiting us from Germany, and he hasn't visited us anymore because he is afraid Jamie will knock him down again."

Her granny lifted Amy onto her knee and cuddled her, "oh my lovely sweet girl, everything will be ok when your daddy comes to visit. Jamie has promised not to fight with daddy again and your daddy will be good and not shout at mummy. So, don't worry about anything now and maybe draw daddy a nice picture that your mummy can send to him. What do you say to that?"

After her granny's explanation, Amy got down and with a cheery smile she went off to draw a picture saying over her shoulder, "that's a good idea and I will draw a special one."

When Amy had left the room, her dad suggested that Jenny should have a word with Jamie and get him to understand it isn't wise to be angry with Roy for the sake of the children. Jenny was in agreement and she had a quiet moment of reflection thinking what an awful mess this divorce was and how on earth was she going to explain to the children when it was finally over and she would no longer be together with their daddy.

She was brought out of her thoughts by mum suggesting they all get ready and had a picnic in the park to give the children some pleasure and prevent the adults from thinking about the problem of Roy.

At the park, the children fed the ducks and Charlie danced around with excitement when a beautiful swan decided to land on the water and, scattering the ducks, was gobbling up the bread that had been thrown into the water. Jenny rushed forward and, like the protective mother she was, she grabbed hold of Charlie's arm pulling him away from the edge of the water. "Whoa Charlie, not so close or you will end up swimming with the ducks in the water!"

Charlie began to chuckle at his mother's words and replied "Silly mummy."

Everyone began to laugh and at last the mood was lightened and they all had a good time being together, enjoying all that the park had to offer, including an ice cream which had kept the children sitting still for the first time since they had come into the park.

On arriving back home, there was just the tea to prepare then after a bedtime story, the children would settle down to sleep. Before that though, Amy had to finish her drawing, colouring it in, desperately trying to keep within the lines. When at last it was completed, Amy gave the picture to her mummy making her promise she would send it the very next day to her daddy. Jenny was surprised by Charlie who had also attempted to do a drawing and insisted that Jenny also sent it with the one from Amy to his daddy. This made the tears well up in Jenny's eyes as she once again had thoughts that she might break her children's hearts when the divorce was final. Then she was reminded that she had to fight Roy for custody first, but she didn't want to dwell on that just now, so taking both children in hand they proceeded to the table where her mother had laid on a lovely tea.

CHAPTER 18

Jamie came to visit the following evening, bringing some colouring books for the children, who were excited when he told them he would read a bedtime story. Later, over a cup of coffee, Jenny showed him the letters. He eagerly read them and afterwards told Jenny how really sorry he was to read what she had to cope with while living with Roy. However, he was in agreement with her that the letters would go a long way to proving what Roy's behaviour was like and what she had to deal with, trying to keep the marriage going whilst protecting the children from the violence that was occurring.

He left after chatting to her parents for a short time, telling them he would write a letter also to confirm that there was no romance between him and Jenny, so that Roy's accusation of adultery would be shown to be untrue. Jenny's parents stated that they would be writing a letter also as a character reference for their daughter and also showing how much she had relaxed since coming to live with them. All this talk of support for her put Jenny in a positive frame of mind that she just might stop Roy from claiming custody of her children.

Two days later, her parents and Jamie had both handed Jenny the promised letters to add to the ones from Renata and the SSAFA Sister. By the afternoon she had made an appointment to see Mr Benson at the solicitor's office and would be seeing him a week later, giving her time to organise the time off work.

The following Saturday, Jenny took the children to visit her friend Mary. The children were extra excited to have a playdate with Martin who they had not seen for a month. Mary didn't visit very often due to Jenny working and usually being out with her parents and occasionally with Jamie at the weekends. So it was with a happy mood that Jenny greeted Mary and gave a big hug to Martin too. Just as soon as the children were happily playing in the corner of the room, Mary and Jenny sat down with a cup of tea and Mary was eager to hear all the latest news from her friend.

After discussing all the pros and cons about the letters Jenny had in her possession, Mary was pleased that this had brought some positivity to Jenny and she offered to write a letter supporting her friend's character and being a good mother. Jenny was overwhelmed at the support her friend offered but stated that because they had been apart from each other for such a long time, it might not be taken as a character reference, but Jenny said she would speak to Mr Benson and ask if it would be good to have a letter from Mary and she would let her friend know the answer.

***

The meeting with Mr Benson was very informative. Jenny had given him the letters to read and after he was finished his next words pleased her. "Well now Mrs Crabtree, you have been busy collecting evidence and references to your character and that of being a mother to your children. These are well documented and will indeed act to help your case for the divorce and the custody of the children." He paused and reached for a letter out of the file in front of him, "Here is a letter from your husband's solicitor and I will leave you to read this."

Jenny reached across the desk to retrieve the letter and proceeded to read its contents. It was fairly short and to the point and when she had finished reading, she commented to Mr Benson, "It appears my husband is still pursuing the accusation of adultery and is stating he has evidence. However, I cannot see what evidence he could have unless it is hearsay when my alleged adultery never occurred."

"Do not worry yourself over this matter. Mr Crabtree is simply playing for time and if it is just hearsay then this will not be accepted as proof."

"Oh, I am not in the least bit worried about whatever it is he thinks he knows about Jamie and myself. This friend has been very supportive of me and if I were to commit adultery, I couldn't think of anyone in my life better to do that with. However, I can assure you we are just good friends and hope to remain so."

"Good, and as for the matter of your friend Mary also writing a letter, any documentation would be helpful to your case, even someone you work with to state your work ethics would be useful. I will leave that with you to decide what is relevant"

Jenny thanked the solicitor for his time and the

advice before leaving his office to return to her workplace. During the journey there, she reflected on what had been said and wondered if it could be possible someone friendly with Roy was keeping an eye on her and reporting back to him. If that was true, Jenny was adamant in her mind that there wasn't anything to report back to him because Jenny felt she was just getting on with her life and not doing anything wrong that might give Roy ammunition to use against her.

Back at home, after work, her parents were eager to learn what the solicitor had said to Jenny. They were very annoyed to hear that Roy was still accusing Jamie and her of being unfaithful and were quick to question what possible evidence he could have.

Jenny once again reassured them that he couldn't have any evidence because it had never occurred, but she did mention her thoughts of earlier that he was spying on her through someone who knows her and lives close by. They were all then pondering on who that might be, but no one could come up with anyone who knew Roy and Jenny and lived near to them. Later Jenny had an idea and asked her mum if she could look at the photos of her and Roy's wedding.

After spending an hour studying all the photos and dismissing the memories it brought back to her, she remembered that the best man had been a very close friend and drinking buddy to Roy. Could he still be in touch with her husband and would there be any possibility it was he who was spying on her? She made up her mind to find him and where he was living to see if her suspicions could be true. When telling her parents what she was thinking, her dad agreed he would make some discreet enquiries and try to find him but first he needed to know his name from Jenny.

"I remember Roy calling him John Boy, but that would have been his nickname. So maybe his first name is John?" Jenny was now silent, lost in deep thought. Then surprising them all she blurted out, "Johnny Walton! That is his name and that's why Roy called him John Boy after the one in the Waltons drama on the television."

"Are you sure that was his name? Can you be definitely certain and anything else you might remember, such as where he worked when he was friends with Roy?"

"Yes, I remember he worked with his dad who had a plumbing business. His dad was called Mr Dave

Walton and I believe he lived on Derwent Road which is about three streets away from here, but I can't remember what house number he lived at."

"That's a good start and I will visit Derwent Road tomorrow and see if I can find out if he still lives there or anything else that might be useful." Jenny's dad was showing much enthusiasm to help out his daughter.

"If you do that, you will be careful won't you? Please don't get yourself into any trouble and remember this is only a suspicion of mine. I have no proof it could be Johnny."

"Don't you worry yourself. I will be the soul of discretion and hopefully at least I can find out which house he might live in."

Jenny gave her dad a hug and told him he was her rock, "You are the best dad anyone could have and I am so glad to have you supporting me." With that she wished him goodnight and went off to bed hoping she would be able to sleep with all the thoughts whirling around in her head.

CHAPTER 19

In the morning, Jenny was kept busy getting Amy and Charlie's breakfast and then making sure they were properly dressed and ready for granny to take Amy to school accompanied by Charlie. Before leaving the house, herself to go to work, Jenny reminded her dad once again to take care whilst making enquiries about Johnny Walton. Her dad promised he would be careful, so she left for work reassured and hoping Ted might have news for her when she returned.

Arriving home at twelve thirty, she was eager to see if her dad had any news and even before she had removed her coat, she was questioning him. "Did you go to Derwent Road and find anything useful there?"

"Steady on girl, take off your coat and sit down then I will pass on my news."

Jenny did as she was told while her mum made a cup of tea for them both. Jenny asked again if he had news and her mood was excitement mixed with anxiety and Ted could see she would not be satisfied until he passed on his findings.

"Well now, firstly I did go to Derwent Road, and it wasn't difficult to find the correct house where Johnny Walton lives. It was on the corner and was number two and I knew immediately that he must live there. A white van was in the driveway and on the side was written JOHN BOY PLUMBING. "

Jenny sat with her mouth agape, staring, surprised at this revelation. It was a few moments before she could speak. "So, he does live close to us, but is he still friends with Roy I wonder and how on earth are we going to find out?"

"Well, since I returned home, I have been thinking about a way I can find out more about him. The first problem will be to get to speak to him, so, I have decided tomorrow I will go back to his house and knock on the door. He must surely live there or why else would his name be on that van and not his dad's name?"

"What are you going to say to him if it is Johnny Walton who answers the door?" Betty was now questioning her husband with a puzzled look on her face, "surely you can't just ask him outright if he is spying on your daughter?"

"Oh mum, you have a good point there." Jenny was nodding in agreement, "Just what do you intend to do or say to him? Like mum says, you can't just accuse him especially when we don't know if he is still in contact with Roy."

Ted did not answer their question immediately. He sat very still, head bowed and in deep thought. After a while he raised his head and had a huge smile on his face. Jenny instinctively knew he had an answer. "You've thought of something haven't you I can tell by your face that you have an idea?"

"Yes, I have an idea but whether it will work remains to be seen."

"C'mon Ted, don't keep it to yourself. Tell us what you're planning." Betty urged her husband.

"I need to think some more and get everything right in my head about what I should say to him.

Basically, I will go to see him and pretend I am looking for a plumber to do some work for me. Then, when I have his full attention, I will tell him I recognise him."

Jenny was quick to jump in with her doubts, "Won't that give the game away if he also recognises you and questions why you are really there?"

"Oh, he won't recognise me because I plan to disguise myself a bit. I have my reading glasses and a peaked cap and I need to find the artificial moustache I used once for a fancy-dress party and maybe I still have the wig I used then also."

At this point Betty burst out laughing, "Oh, trust you to think of using a disguise you always did love a fancy-dress party."

"That sounds brilliant! If you are able to pull this off that is." Jenny clapped her hands in obvious approval at her dad's plan. "However, you still haven't told us what you plan to say to him after you've told him you recognise him."

"I still need to finalise my questions to him yet, but the idea is to find out if he's still in contact with

Roy."

"That's all very well dad, but you must have the right questions in your head. Maybe I can suggest something. I'm happy to help and I don't want you getting into trouble if you say the wrong thing."

"Jenny is right Ted; you can't just ask him outright if he is spying on her." Betty is looking and sounding anxious.

"Let's have another cup of tea and give ourselves some time to put our thinking caps on and come up with some suggestions. I'll go and make the tea and something to eat because I haven't had any lunch and I'm so hungry."

While Jenny was in the kitchen, Ted found a pen and paper and wrote down his reason for visiting Johnny Walton. He starts with asking him for a quote for work on the bathroom hoping Johnny will ask him inside where he can then suggest that he recognises him.

"What are you writing dad?" Jenny asks on returning with tea from the kitchen. Have you come up with any ideas on how to find out what we need to know?"

"Not really, I have just started with a list and first on it is what I should say if he answers the door."

"Oh, then we must think of your next move to get the answers we need."

They all sat quietly drinking the tea, no one spoke, they were too busy thinking. Suddenly, Jenny spoke excitedly, "After you tell him you recognise him you could then say after a short pause, you were at the wedding of Roy Crabtree. Then depending on his reply, you could ask if he's still in contact with him." Jenny was staring at her dad for his reaction to her suggestions.

"Yes, that's a good idea and if he tells me he is still in contact, I can then ask if he sees much of him because I heard he is in the army and based in Germany. Of course, the continuing conversation will depend on his answers."

"Then, if he does tell you he is in contact with Roy, you could possibly go on to ask if Roy is ok because you have been told by his mum that he is going through a divorce and ask Johnny if he knew this." Jenny's head was a whirl of thoughts, she imagined the conversation between Ted and Johnny Walton.

"You shouldn't appear too prying, it would be best to make it appear chatty, just making conversation. If you know what I mean." Betty, who hadn't spoken until now, was eager to put this point across to her husband.

"Of course dear, I will try my best to act casual, but like I said before, it will depend on what Johnny Walton says to me. So for now, we should leave it there. I promise I'll not mess this up and, all being well, we might have the answer we are looking for."

Jenny didn't get much sleep that night. Too many doubts in her head, worrying if it was the right thing to let her dad go snooping. What sort of person was her dad going to visit? What if her dad said the wrong thing and Johnny Walton wasn't a nice person, then her dad may be in trouble. Oh, why did she agree to this meeting? Perhaps she should put a stop to it after all. What good would it do to find out that he was spying on her? Her mind was in a conflicting mood and, try as she might, she couldn't decide what to do.

When telling her parents she had doubts about dad going to see Johnny, he was quick to reassure her it would be ok and he knew just how to handle the situation. So, Jenny went off to work but not quite yet reassured, with jangled nerves and a feeling of dread, she knew she had to leave this to her dad to deal with knowing he was doing his best to help. At work she confided in her colleague who was always eager to hear how things were for Jenny.

Jane, her colleague and friend worked alongside Jenny in the office. This was the only person at work whom she would tell her troubles to and she knew Jane wasn't a gossip, so whatever she told her would not be passed on. Jane was shocked to learn that Jenny may be being spied on, but she was in full agreement with Jenny's dad that it was a good way to get to the bottom of this and throughout the morning she kept reassuring Jenny that everything would be ok and she should have faith in her dad. By the time Jenny was leaving for home she was so pleased she had a friend like Jane.

Arriving home, Jenny was welcomed by a beaming smile on her dad's face and acting like the cat that got the cream. Throwing down her coat, she quickly went to her dad's side and, looking him straight in his eyes, she begged him to tell her what had happened during his visit. Ted could wait no longer as he was bursting to tell his daughter the good news he had.

"We were right! Johnny Walton has been keeping in touch with Roy. He told me this and that's not all. He also told me he was in a bit of a state over what to do because Roy had asked him to keep an eye on you and let him know what you were getting up to."

"Oh, that's good news and did he confess to telling Roy I had committed adultery?"

"That's not all he told me. He only mentioned to your husband that he had seen you at a restaurant with a man. Afterwards, Roy wanted him to keep following you, but he has refused to do that and now he is sorry that he ever got involved with Roy and his divorce. Johnny says he has told Roy he won't spy on you and only wants to stay mates if Roy can accept this. Since then, he hasn't heard from Roy again."

"So, Roy is trying to cause trouble by telling his Solicitor I have committed adultery. I can now let Mr Benson know that Roy has put two and two together and believed I did because a friend saw me with Jamie when we went out for a meal. This should put a spanner in the works. It will mean he cannot counteract my accusation of his abuse of me. Maybe this will show how devious and a liar he is and possibly show he cannot be trusted to get custody of the children." She gave her dad a big hug and kissed his cheek, so pleased her dad came through for her.

Betty asked Ted if the young man had recognised him, but before he could answer she also asked him how he got Johnny Walton to tell him all this?

"Oh, it was really easy. I didn't have to question him much and before I knew it, he was telling me all about his dealings with Roy. I found him to be a nice lad, not at all how I imagined him and I almost felt sorry for him when he told me his friendship with Roy was coming to an end after all the years they had been mates. All because Roy was being a nuisance and pressuring him to do his dirty work. He genuinely appeared upset, but I tried to reassure him that it would be best not to have any communication with Roy, then he couldn't be demanding."

"It appears that Roy has just been using him and the poor thing didn't want to be involved. At least we know now what the situation is, thank God." Betty appeared to be annoyed at what had been going on.

Flopping back into the chair Jenny let out a big sigh and couldn't stop the tears from rolling down her cheeks. They were tears of happiness and relief that at last she knew Roy wouldn't be able to state she had been unfaithful. It wasn't over though and she knew she must stay strong and stop him getting his hands on the children.

CHAPTER 20

After Jenny had informed Mr Benson of what had been happening, explaining how Roy was getting information, he was happy for her that the real truth was out and he promised her he would be contacting her husband's solicitor very soon. He told her to just get on with her life for now, but contact him if she had any further news she wanted to discuss. They ended their conversation on a happy note when he praised her and Ted for their detective work.

She made her mind up that she would get on with her life and not worry about the divorce proceedings. Jane, her work friend, was so pleased when Jenny told her all the happenings of the last few days. To Jenny's surprise, Jane asked her if she would like to go with her to a local dance? Jenny replied that she would but first she will need to speak to her parents about looking after Amy and Charlie. Jenny said she would let Jane know the next day, reassuring her friend that she was almost sure it would be ok.

Just as Jenny had predicted, her parents thought it was a great idea for her to get out and enjoy herself. At work, Jenny told Jane she would go with her and asked for the details of the venue. It was at the community hall, within walking distance for Jenny and it was this Saturday and they arranged to meet outside the hall at seven thirty. Jenny went home from work in a very happy mood but it was not to last.

Betty handed Jenny a letter and it was postmarked Germany so she knew without opening it that it was from Roy. There was a quizzical look on Betty's face, as she too had decided who it was from and Jenny could tell from this look that she was wanting to find out what Roy had written. Both women sat close on the sofa and with trembling hands Jenny tore open the envelope.

It wasn't a long letter but it was a polite request that Roy should be allowed to visit Amy and Charlie and possibly take them out for the day. This was to be in a week's time while he was home from Germany visiting his mother and of course the children if that could be arranged. Jenny read the letter out loud so her mum, who was waiting patiently by her side, knew what he had written.

It had been over four months since Roy last visited but, although she wished it wasn't so, she would have to let him see the children. As for taking them out for the day she was concerned. Could she trust him? She had only taken the children twice to see their other grandma, so if Roy was wanting to take them to her house, she supposed that would be ok. As soon as the children were in bed, Jenny wrote a short letter to Roy telling him that the children would be looking forward to his visit and stating that she would be at work so wouldn't see him but her parents would have the children ready for him.

The week passed too quickly for Jenny. She had a good time at the dance with Jane where a local band had provided the music. Jenny had a lot of dance partners from the many single lads there, but it was only fun and she returned home happy and de-stressed. It was the best night's sleep she had in a long time. Jamie came round on Sunday and they took the children to the park. Amy and Charlie happily played in the sand pit while the adults sat on a bench and chatted.

"It's so good to see you again," Jenny said, "I've missed you popping round to dads."

"I did think of you while I was away on my course. Three weeks seemed to drag on and I couldn't wait to get home and hear all your news."

"There is lots to tell you. It's all been happening here, so much excitement and I have even been out on the Town." Jenny gave a little laugh at her description of going to the dance.

"Yes, I heard. You've been raving it up at the community hall. I only hope you behaved yourself and your dancing didn't embarrass anyone."

"Oh you! I'll have you know my dancing is great and I did behave myself and found it enjoyable if you must know." Jenny was putting on a face like she was offended, but Jamie said he was only joking with her. "Did you also hear of how my dad got to the bottom of who was spying on me?"

"No, but please tell me, tell me everything that has been happening."

Jenny began her story of dad visiting Johnny Walton and him being a friend of her husband. She ended by telling Jamie what Johnny had told her dad and that she had passed the information on to Mr Benson, her solicitor. Jamie, with a huge smile on his face, told Jenny he was amazed at their cunning way of getting this information and that he hoped that this would stop Roy from accusing her of cheating on him. She assured him that it should, but they would just have to wait and see. After a pause to check on the children, Jenny then broke the news to Jamie that Roy would be visiting that coming week and taking the children out for the day.

"That's not so good news! Do you want me to come round just in case he kicks off at you again? Jamie appeared really concerned for Jenny.

"That is very kind of you to offer, but it will not be necessary because I'll be at work and my parents will see to him. So, I won't see him until he brings the children home and even then, I aim to keep out of the way and let my dad take control.

"I'm glad about that." The sound of relief in Jamie's voice was clear. "After what happened last time he visited, I am concerned for you and don't want you to get hurt."

"No need to worry, my parents have everything planned to hopefully have a more pleasant visit."

They both became silent, lost in their thoughts until Charlie came up to them stating he wanted to have ice cream. Jamie whisked him up onto his knee and tickled Charlie's tummy,. playfully asking if his tummy was ready for all that ice cream? Charlie, while wriggling and giggling out loud, insisted it would fit a big one in his tummy. With that answer, how could they deny him, so Jenny called Amy to come as they were leaving. Amy reluctantly left the side of her friend she had been chatting to but cheered up when ice cream was mentioned. On the way home Jenny asked Jamie about his course and how he got on away from home. All too soon they were outside her parent's house and Jamie left her promising to come see her the following evening.

Jamie kept his promise and he read the children a bedtime story. Afterwards, the adults discussed Roy's visit the next day. Ted assured Jamie that he would take no bad behaviour from Roy and if he should kick off, Betty would call the police. Jamie was pleased to hear this and an hour later he went home, with a promise to come again the next evening to find out if all went well.

***

It was Thursday, Jenny was up early and had gotten the children dressed ready for the day out. She hadn't yet told them that their daddy was coming to visit as she didn't want them getting too excited. Although, once Jenny had shared the news, Amy was indeed very excited, jumping up and down and going round in circles until at last she calmed down and took up a position by the front window to watch out for her daddy arriving.

Jenny had explained she would still have to go to work. So, after telling the children to be good for their grandparents and to enjoy their day out, she left to head to her workplace. With a pounding heart and thoughts all over the place, she admonished herself to calm down because her parents had everything under control. Once at work and with reassurance from her friend Jane, she tried to concentrate on her work and get through the morning until the time arrived to go home.

Her feet hardly touched the ground as she hurried towards home, eager to ask her parents how things went when Roy arrived to take the children. Happy when being told that all went well, Roy was polite and hugged the children. Less than half an hour later, he was gone with his two excited children in tow. Jenny could finally relax.

CHAPTER 21

The rest of the day Jenny kept herself busy tidying the children's bedroom and then her own bedroom. The time appeared to drag on slowly, but maybe it could have been because Jenny frequently checked her watch. She stopped and made tea for herself and her parents, who were equally on edge and trying hard to talk about anything other than the impending return of Roy with the children. He had told them that he would return by six that evening and Jenny had agreed with her dad that she should make herself scarce and perhaps go into her bedroom to avoid any confrontation with Roy.

Six o clock arrived at last but by seven there was still no sign of Roy. Another half an hour passed and Jamie had arrived hoping to find out how the children's day had been. Instead, he had his work cut out trying to calm Jenny, who by now was almost hysterical with worry that something bad may have happened. Betty was busying herself making yet another pot of tea and Ted made frequent visits to the window to check for the intended arrival of Roy with the children.

By eight, Jenny and her dad were travelling to Roy's mother's house to find out if Roy was with her. Arriving outside the house, Jenny could hardly contain herself until her dad applied the brake and she was out of the car door and up the garden path to the front door. It wasn't a polite knocking but more of a banging on the door and when his mother opened it, Jenny pushed past her, almost knocking her over.

"Well, come in, why don't you?" Roy's mother said. "What is going on? You're acting like someone's been murdered?"

"Where is he and where are my children?" Jenny, by now was beside herself with both fear and anger.

"If you mean Roy, I thought you knew where he was with the children. He told me you knew he was planning to go to the seaside with Amy and Charlie. Wanted me to go too but my legs are playing me up, it's the arthritis you know."

"The seaside!" Jenny's voice was raised, showing her surprise at what she just heard. "When... Where did he take them? I didn't agree to anything like that!"

"Oh dear, then he was telling me a lie because he said he was going there for a few days and that you were pleased he was going." Mrs Crabtree was now looking very worried, her face screwed up showing many wrinkles.

"How long has he gone there for and when did he say he would be back?" Jenny had calmed down somewhat and now was needing more details. She was having difficulty getting her head around what Roy had done, especially when he hadn't asked her permission to do this.

Jenny's dad had so far remained quiet since they arrived but now, he too started to question Roy's mother for details of just when Roy intended to return. "Has your son told you when he is coming home?" He tried very hard to stay calm.

Mrs Crabtree looked over to where Ted was standing and in a quiet voice she said, "he said he was only going for three days, so I am expecting him to come home the day after tomorrow. They've only gone to Blackpool so it won't take them long to get back.

Jenny, who was now sitting down trying to calm herself, jumped to her feet on hearing where Roy had gone with her children. "Dad, we'll have to go there and bring the children back with us," Then turning to Mrs Crabtree, "Do you know where they were going to be staying, a B & B or hotel perhaps?"

"He didn't tell me that Jenny, honestly, he didn't. I only know it was Blackpool." Mrs Crabtree now got hold of Jenny's hand, "Amy and Charlie are with their dad so they won't come to any harm, he will look after them, believe me."

"I know he is their dad but don't you know how worried I've been wondering why he didn't return them to me at six? He had no right to just take them without first discussing this with me."

At this point Ted decided to offer some advice to his daughter. "Come on Jenny, Let's get off home, there is nothing we can do. It's no use going after him when we don't know where they are staying. We can only be patient and wait for him to bring the children back to you. We have to trust he will look after them."

Jenny didn't feel ready to go home yet, her anger had risen and she wanted to punish Roy. "I don't want to go home, but I would like to go to the police station and report him for stealing my children!"

"Now now Jenny, you're not thinking straight. You are upset and angry, I know, but we must be sensible and think about this. What will the police do when they know Amy and Charlie are with their daddy and he has just taken them to the seaside for some fun?"

"But he didn't tell me he was going to do this. Surely they will see it from my point of view?"

"That may be so, but he has never hurt the children and you don't have permanent custody of the children yet. All they will probably see is that Roy is a soldier home on leave and wants to spend time with his children. You have no evidence that he will harm them so we have no choice other than to wait until the day after tomorrow and if he doesn't return then, we can inform the police. Don't you think that is your best option?"

"Maybe you are right about what the police will think, but you know Roy can be violent. He has a temper and I don't trust him."

"I know just how you feel but you must be patient. I'm sure he will bring them back safe; he loves them and they love him and are probably having a great time in Blackpool. So please, stay calm and let's go home."

Jenny, shrugging her shoulders, finally agreed with her dad and with a hug for Mrs Crabtree they both left and got into the car to return home. Although her angry mood was gone, she was showing the distress she was feeling when the tears spilled over her cheeks and she covered her face with her hands.

Once home and still tearful, Jenny tried to convey all that they had found out from Roy's mother. Jamie rushed to Jenny's side and with his arms wrapped around her he tried to comfort her. Believing everything could be solved by a nice cuppa, Betty once again went off to make a pot of tea.

Eventually Jenny dried her eyes and was quiet. Jamie had suggested she should try not to worry and, whatever she thought about Roy's deceitfulness, she should instead think about the nice holiday Amy and Charlie are having with their dad and although she missed them terribly, to stay positive that it would all be all right in the end. Jenny was comforted by Jamie's words and she promised to try to relax and look forward to the day after tomorrow when she would be reunited with her children.

When finally alone in her bed, it was not quite as easy to stay positive and the more she thought about what had happened, the more she worried that Roy was looking after Amy and Charlie. The tears made another appearance and she cried herself to sleep, exhausted after a stressful day.

How to get by over the next two days? That was the question Jenny thought of as she awoke from her restless sleep. Pondering whether maybe she could stay in bed with the covers wrapped over her head and ignore anyone who invaded her space. She decided that was a ludicrous idea and so she finally got out of bed, dressed herself and went slowly down the stairs.

It was strange not having the children there to get them breakfast and check that Charlie had put his shoes on the correct feet which he nearly always hadn't, or Amy's constant chatter, and questioning about all manner of things. She felt alone and was trying very hard to keep her mind positive. Somehow, she would have to keep herself busy for the next two days whether she liked it or not.

While trying to eat some cereal, she allowed herself to wonder what the children would be doing. Would they be missing her and had Charlie got over his shyness with his daddy? Perhaps Amy would look after Charlie, she often did, showing a nice caring side to her especially where her little brother was concerned.

Her parents came into the kitchen and Betty put the kettle on to make tea. She was good at making tea and also keeping busy so she wouldn't dwell too much on her grandchildren not being there. Ted sat down at the table and stroked his daughter's arm. He too looked lost and much quieter than his usual self. "What have you got planned for today, Jenny? Will you be going to work or taking the day off? I'll phone in for you and say you're not well"

Immediately his daughter answered him, "Yes, I think I'll go to work. It will help me to take my mind off the children and afterwards I thought I would visit Mary as I haven't been to see her recently."

"Well, if you're sure that's what you want to do

and I'm sure Mary will be happy to see you."

"So, we'll see you at teatime will we?" Without waiting for an answer her mum carried on speaking, "I'll make you a nice tea, bake a cake and get some ham for sandwiches. Perhaps we'll have a trifle too." Betty appeared happy at her suggestion.

"That would be very nice, mum. I'll be home at about four and now I must get myself ready for work." With this Jenny went to ready herself for the day ahead, promising herself that she would try to cheer up and only telling her friend Jane the bare minimum information about what had happened.

Just before she left home, Jamie came round to see how she was feeling. Jenny told him she had missed having the children there this morning but that she was doing her best to stay positive. He was pleased to hear she was going to work and then going to visit Mary after which he had to leave to go to work also. Before he did leave, Betty asked if he would like to come to tea when he got home from his day's work. She told him how she was planning a nice tea to cheer them all up. Jamie accepted the invite and told her he would come round about five to five thirty depending on the traffic of his journey home.

"That's agreed then, we shall see you later for tea and afterwards we could all play Monopoly. That should keep us busy until bedtime." Ted came up with this idea to keep their minds off missing the children. It was all arranged and so Jamie went off to his workplace and Jenny left to get the bus to the warehouse where she worked.

CHAPTER 22

The morning dragged on for Jenny. At morning coffee break she sat down with Jane and explained that the children had gone to Blackpool with Roy and were due back home the next day. At first, Jane had thought this was good until Jenny then told her she hadn't been aware this was going to happen because Roy was supposed to only be having them for the day. With this further information, Jane gasped and then said how that was a terrible thing to do to her friend. She then asked Jenny how she felt about this.

"At first, I was anxious for the safety of Amy and Charlie, then I became angry and wanted to go and fetch them home. My dad talked sense into me and made me realise that Blackpool was a big place and we had no idea where Roy was staying with the children."

"I bet you were angry; I would have been too. So,

what did you do in the end?" Jane was eager to hear more.

"Well, we had to go home. You see, we only found out about this when we visited Mrs Crabtree, Roy's mother. She was also angry that I hadn't known about her son's plans. He had told her he had my permission to take them away."

"Didn't she know where they intended to stay. Maybe a bed and breakfast? There are loads of them in Blackpool. I know because me and my hubby stayed in a few over the years."

"No, she said she had no knowledge of that. So, we had two options, go to the police or go back home and wait for his return. My dad was adamant we shouldn't go to the police. Not yet anyway and after his explanation why, I agreed to go home."

Jane hung on every word Jenny had to say and told her she was very brave to come to work, telling her she would have been in pieces and unable to think of anything else let alone working here. Jenny explained how the idea was that work would keep her busy and help keep her mind off what had happened. Then, Jenny reminded Jane they needed to get back to work or they would be in trouble. The rest of the morning was very busy sorting out two customers' problems with the machine parts they had received, which were both incorrect and needed to be resent.

At last, home time came for Jenny and she walked slowly on her way to Mary's home. Her thoughts were of what she would say to Roy when he finally brought the children home and should she remain calm or be really angry with him?

Maybe, she decided, it would be best to remain calm while her parents got the children settled. Then afterwards she could let her anger out and tell Roy just what she thought of him. It occurred to her then that she had no idea just what time of day Roy intended to bring Amy and Charlie home. Jenny decided there and then that if he hadn't made an appearance by five, she would go to the police and report him.

Arriving at her friend's house, Mary was so pleased to see her and gave her a big hug. Mary told Jenny that Martin was having his afternoon nap but that she would be able to see him before she left again.

When sat at the table in the kitchen, Jenny was surprised to find a Victoria sponge cake and cups and saucers ready for their tea. "Oh Mary, you shouldn't have gone to all this trouble. I am assuming you baked this cake? It looks delicious."

"Yes, I baked it, but no trouble because it gave me something to do. I have a lot of spare time now that Martin is older and amuses himself playing with his toys. Pour lamb doesn't get many other children to play with."

"That's a shame and I am sorry Amy and Charlie are not here with me to play with him."

"It's ok, really it is. I believe you came after finishing work and that Amy is at school anyway."

Jenny was quiet for a while, lost in her thoughts and Mary asked if everything was ok with her.

"I am sorry." Jenny said, "I'm not myself today. Amy isn't at school and Charlie is not at home. You see Roy has taken them to Blackpool for a few days. They went yesterday, but I didn't know until yesterday evening after visiting his mother to find out why he hadn't brought the children back home." Her tears spilled over her cheeks, the stress becoming all too clear now.

Mary had a shocked look on her face and appeared stunned. Then she sprang into action and put her arms around her friend to comfort her. "Oh Jenny, what a thing for him to do! He had no right to just take them away without discussing it with you. I'm not surprised you're upset. When is he coming back and returning the children to you?"

Between sobs Jenny managed to tell Mary how she hoped he was returning tomorrow but at what time she had no idea. Hugging her friend more tightly, Mary felt helpless to say or do anything to comfort Jenny. After a while with Mary's arms around her, Jenny's tears subsided and she became calm. "I'm sorry for getting upset. I've been trying so hard to remain positive but it has been difficult. I keep thinking, what if he doesn't bring them back and what if he has taken them to Germany?"

"No, he couldn't do that. Surely you still have their passports? The children wouldn't be able to leave the country without them. Don't worry yourself about that sort of thing. I'm sure he isn't stupid enough to keep them with him for longer when he must be scheduled to return himself to Germany and back to the army." Mary was trying desperately to help her friend to see sense.

"I'm sure you're right Mary. He would be very foolish to keep hold of them. I intend to speak to the police anyway, if he doesn't return by tomorrow teatime."

"That's my girl! You just keep thinking like that and everything will sort itself out. Now, let's have a cup of tea and a piece of cake before Martin wakes up from his nap."

After Martin made an appearance, Jenny cuddled him. He then brought one toy after another to show how pleased he was to have someone to play with. Jenny then had an idea and suggested to Mary that maybe Martin would enjoy going to a nursery maybe for a couple of mornings during the week. She told her friend all about Amy going to Kindergarten in Germany, explaining that it was a type of playschool there and how much her daughter enjoyed it.

Mary showed an interest in this suggestion, stating that she felt sure he would like that but asking if maybe he was too young to go to nursery. Jenny reassured her that nurseries took children from babies up to school age. Mary said she would make some enquiries, adding that if Martin settled in at a nursery, maybe she would go back to work for the mornings he was there, giving her a chance to spend time doing something for herself. Jenny thought that was a good idea. She only worked in the mornings so couldn't see why Mary couldn't also.

The friends said their goodbyes at three thirty and Jenny felt much better after spending time with Mary and Martin. On her way home, she decided that she would not mope around the next day, which was Saturday, but would ask her mum to go into town with her. It was about time she had a new dress and this would cheer her up.

CHAPTER 23

Saturday dawned with bright sunshine and the two women were off to the town centre to do some shopping. Ted dropped them off in his car and they arranged to catch the bus back home when they were ready. It had been an enjoyable morning, just the two of them with no children in tow. Jenny not only bought a new dress but also some shoes and a toy each for Amy and Charlie to welcome them home.

To keep busy during the afternoon she had decided to write letters to her solicitor, Renata and the SSAFA sister. After finishing the solicitor's letter describing what Roy had been up to, she had lots more to write about to the other two. Ted took the letters to the post box for her while she helped her mum prepare the tea.

At four thirty, Roy arrived, bringing the children

back home. He wasn't invited in and Betty took the children inside so that Jenny could have words with Roy. He wasn't apologetic for taking the children away without asking Jenny first and stated that he only decided to take them to the seaside later after he had collected them on Thursday. Not sure whether to believe him, she calmly asked him if he cared how anxious she was when he didn't appear at six on that day and she had no idea where he was or what he had done. Roy only smiled and then stated that now she knew how he had felt when she took them back to England and away from him.

Jenny was amazed at this and could feel her anger rising even though she'd promised herself she wouldn't get angry. For a few moments, she didn't know how to respond to his comments, then she let her anger show as she said, "How dare you use the children to get back at me. They have nothing to do with why we are separated!"

Her voice was rising, "You are to blame for me leaving you and Germany. I couldn't get far enough away from your terrible behaviour, and taking the children was to keep them safe and protect them from the atmosphere you were creating in our marriage."

Roy stared at her; his lips tight with an angry look. "Oh, yes you would blame me. It was obvious to me that you were not one bit sorry for the humiliation you caused me. Calling the police because you couldn't take a joke. Then you went and humiliated me all over again by going to see my commanding officer." He continued to stare at her with a steely glare.

"Well, I might have known you wouldn't see that you're drinking and violent behaviour would cause our marriage to break down. Saying sorry each time you hit me wasn't enough. It was just a word you thought would excuse your behaviour."

"It wasn't all me. You were only interested in the children. I was becoming just a wage earner for you. If you had paid more attention to me then maybe I wouldn't have lashed out at you, trying to get your attention." Roy was still in denial that his behaviour was to blame.

Jenny was suddenly feeling emotional and a tear rolled down her cheek. "I loved you and I followed you when you joined the army. It was difficult to leave my friends and parents to an unknown future, but I did it because you were my husband and I loved you very much." Jenny could not hold her emotions back and although her tears were flowing faster, she carried on and let out all the hurt she had felt finishing then and now, "I no longer feel that love for you, I can only feel contempt that you are still trying to hurt me and using the children as your weapon to do it." Only now did she become silent and bowed her head so as not to look at him anymore.

Roy stood there quiet, staring at his wife. Something inside him had turned his thoughts to how their marriage had been in that first year and the joy they had both felt when Amy came into their lives. He now was realising that he had destroyed all that and it wasn't Jenny's fault at all. She had been a good wife and mother and he had ruined their marriage by feeling sorry for himself and turning to drink. Should he try one more time to apologise and beg her forgiveness. Was their marriage over and he had lost her and the children? He decided he had to try.

"Please don't cry Jenny, I love you and I now realise what harm I have done. I am sorry, please forgive me. I know that our marriage is over but for the sake of the children please could we still be friends? Saying sorry will never be enough, but I will change I promise. I want to be a good father to Amy and Charlie and I don't want there to be this hatred between us."

Drying her eyes, Jenny wasn't sure that Roy meant what he had just told her but seeing the sadness in his eyes and the way he was looking at her, she hoped he really did mean it and he was at last sorry for his actions in causing the marriage breakdown.

"I need time to think about that. I don't know if I can trust you. You will need to show me by your actions that you really can change." She wasn't ready to forgive and forget just yet, but hoped there might be a turning point. She didn't let Roy know then if they could be friends but instead called out to her mum to bring the children to her.

When Amy and Charlie were by her side, she told them that daddy was leaving to go back to Germany, so they needed to give him a big hug and say goodbye for now. Amy, always questioning, asked her daddy if he would be coming again? When he replied yes, but in a few months' time, she ran to him and gave him a big hug and Charlie did the same.

Jenny became tearful again. It was heartbreaking to see just how much the children loved their daddy.

Would they ever get used to only seeing him now and then? She had no answer to that, but knew there would be no going back to Roy, so it was up to her to help them accept the way the future would be.

CHAPTER 24

In the days and weeks following, life returned to a somewhat normal daily routine. The children went off to school with their granny each morning, Jenny went to work and then collected the children after school. Meanwhile, Ted kept busy making a tree house for his grandkids and, with help from Jamie in the evenings and weekends, it was almost finished.

Roy had written letters to the children and they in turn, with their mummy's help, had drawn and coloured pictures to send back to him. Amy was learning to write at school and so she also wrote a short letter, allowing Charlie to scribble at the bottom of the letter. Jenny was pleased so far that Roy was trying.

Mary, with Martin, had visited and was eager to hear any news from Jenny. Martin was enjoying going to the nursery two mornings a week and so Mary had time to herself even though for just a short time. Jenny had also taken the time to write to Renata and the SSAFA Sister with updates of the events from a few weeks ago. She had yet to hear back from them, certain that she would soon.

Jamie was at the house almost every day and he helped Jenny to take her mind off her problems. Encouraged by her work friend, Jane, Jenny had been out for a meal with Jamie and to the pictures to see a James Bond film. Both were great fans of these films. Her mum was so pleased to see her daughter much more relaxed, and she secretly believed Jamie's company had something to do with it. So, she invited Jamie round for tea on several occasions and even for a Sunday roast dinner.

***

It was halfway through the second year of Jenny and Roy's separation and a letter arrived for Jenny from her solicitor. In it he requested that, if possible, she should visit him in his office the following week on Tuesday afternoon.

She arrived fifteen minutes before the time of her appointment and so waited outside the solicitor's offices to waste some time, however, Mr Benson had been out to lunch and arriving back at his office, he saw Jenny outside the main entrance and promptly invited her in before her appointed time.

After suggesting she should make herself comfortable on the chair in front of his desk, and after she had seated herself, Mr Benson offered her some tea to drink which his secretary had kindly made after seeing them both arrive at the office together. Some secretaries might think this suspicious, the boss going out to lunch and arriving back with a client, an attractive one as well, but not Mrs Stubbs, she respected Mr Benson and was sure her boss would never dally with a young lady behind his wife's back.

They drank their tea in silence, then Mr Benson produced a letter and handed it to Jenny. Reading the contents she was taken by surprise at what it contained. It was from Roy's solicitor and full of good news. Jenny had to read it twice to fully take in what was written. The solicitor was letting Mr Benson know that Mr Roy Crabtree would not be contesting the divorce accusations, nor would he be applying for custody of Amy and Charlie Crabtree.

After allowing Jenny to absorb the contents of the

letter, he began by telling her that this was very good news for the application from her to obtain a divorce from her husband. The divorce proceedings could now go to court unhindered by her husband who was admitting he was in the wrong and giving up any rights to sole custody of his children. This made Jenny a very happy woman. She hadn't had many good things happening in her life lately and this was just the news she needed. Mr Benson was intrigued to know if Jenny had any part in causing this turnaround of her husband's admissions.

Reluctantly, Jenny told her solicitor all about the saga of the Blackpool issue and then how Roy had appeared to suddenly have a conscience about the breakup of their marriage and how he had begged Jenny to forgive him. Once again saying sorry, but this time differently and after the news she had just received, Jenny was beginning to believe he really meant it at last.

Mr Benson listened intently to Jenny, occasionally making a disgruntled tut tutting. Afterwards he said that he too was happy about the letter and had wanted her to read it for herself instead of him telling her of its contents. He again told her the preparations for the divorce hearing would go ahead quite quickly now, but she would not be required to attend the court unless of course she wanted to. She told him that she had no desire to go to the court, so he advised her that she would be hearing from him by letter which would probably be requesting her to visit him again to collect her divorce papers.

Jenny thanked Mr Benson for all his help over the past eighteen months and told him she would be eagerly awaiting to hear from him again. With their goodbyes said, she left his office a happier woman than when she arrived. Before catching the bus home, she called at the bakery and bought the biggest cream cakes they had, one each for the family to celebrate with. Then clutching the precious cake box, she boarded the bus for home eager to tell her parents the good news.

On arriving at home, she could hardly contain her joy and immediately her parents knew she had some good news at last. Jenny assured them that she did have good news but didn't want to tell them in front of the children so they would just have to wait until the children were tucked up in bed. Everyone enjoyed their cream cake and poor Charlie's nose and chin were covered in cream by the time he could eat his. As usual, inquisitive Amy wanted to know why they were having a treat and so granddad told her mummy had good news today, so they were celebrating with a cake. He then asked Amy if she enjoyed her treat and she replied that she wished they could have a treat like that one every week. Granddad told her that treats like that were for special days, but that he would see about more treats if there were any special days soon.

Jenny's parents were delighted with her news, especially Betty who had been dreading Roy winning custody of her grandchildren. No amount of reassurance from her husband that it wouldn't happen hadn't eased Betty's mind, but now she could relax and just enjoy having Jenny and the children with her for a while yet.

Jane was also happy that Jenny's husband had at last seen some sense and admitted his wrong doing. Jane reminded her friend that soon her divorce would come through and she would be a free single woman and maybe just maybe her friendship with Jamie could progress to something more.

The following weekend, Jenny decided to visit Mary to tell her about her good news. Mary was a bit surprised to see her friend but was happy to see her, especially, when over a cup of coffee and cake, Mary heard all about the letter Jenny had read at her solicitors office.

"I am so pleased for you Jenny. How long now before it goes to court?" Mary sounded eager to know.

"Well, Mr Benson said it would go to court soon and that I didn't have to attend, but that he would write to me afterwards."

"So you will very soon be divorced! I know you will be a lot happier after this is finally over with."

"You have no idea how the waiting has been. I have tried not to worry about it, but couldn't help getting anxious, especially not knowing what would be the result of custody of the children. Now I feel like a huge weight has been lifted off my shoulders." Jenny felt tearful but they were tears of relief.

Mary remained silent for a while, then she promptly announced she had some news of her own and without hesitation she told Jenny she was pregnant again, to which Jenny took a huge intake of breath showing her surprise at this news.

"Oh Mary, I am so pleased for you and your husband. You both must be so happy and Martin will have a sibling to play with." Jenny quickly put her arms around Mary and gave her a big hug."We have both got good news, so we should celebrate. I know what we could do. You and your husband, and of course Martin, should come to my home and we'll have a lovely tea party. How does that sound?"

"It sounds great to me and I will bake cakes. So when will this be, have you decided?

"I think next Saturday will be a good day to have it. Do you think that would be alright for you?"

"Yes, we can come on that day. So that's final, we will come to your home around 3 o'clock if that suits you."

Jenny was very thoughtful on the journey home. She did not expect to be told that Mary was pregnant nor that she had a tea party to arrange. She only hoped her parents would be on board with her plans and as she suspected they were when she related her plans for a celebration party after arriving home.

CHAPTER 25

The next week went by in a whirl. Jenny invited Jane to the tea on Saturday and she was happy to accept. When Saturday came around, everyone sat down to a lovely tea with all manner of good things to eat and the celebration cake Mary had made was delicious.

The weekend went by so quickly and Jenny was back at work on Monday. It was a busy day but not too busy for Jenny to attend her bosses office when summoned. She was a bit confused as to why she should be called to see the boss, Mr Nelson. Her nerves were on edge when she entered the office as she stood opposite him.

"Please sit down Jenny, may I call you Jenny?" he pointed to the chair on the opposite side of his huge desk and Jenny promptly did as he asked at the same time replying that she didn't mind if he called her by her name.

"Well now Jenny, you must be wondering why I have called you to come and see me. I can assure you that you have done nothing wrong. On the contrary, I have been checking up on you and have had very favourable reports that you are an excellent employee."

Jenny sat silently with her hands tightly clasped on her lap to stop them trembling. Mr Nelson then went on to state why he wanted to see her. He started by telling her his Secretary was soon to retire and he would need someone to take her place and look after his needs in the office. It would be big shoes to fill he was quick to say, but that he believed Jenny could fit the job if she was willing to take it on.

She was astounded! Never would she have believed when she came to work that morning she was going to be offered the job of being secretary to the boss. Almost immediately she told Mr Nelson she would certainly like to take the job offered but was quick to point out she had not been a secretary before and although she was good on a typewriter she had never learned shorthand.

Mr Nelson kindly put her at ease and told her he knew about her typing course and that she was proficient at that. Then he pointed out that he liked to write his letters longhand to then be typed up. So no shorthand was needed and that any note taking can be in her own way and he would make sure she could keep up with him.

This relieved her anxieties about taking on the job and she was certain she could do whatever the job entailed. Mr Benson then went on to tell Jenny if she started tomorrow she would have a month with Freda, his secretary, to learn the ropes. He also told her that he would be away himself for two weeks which would make it easier on Jenny.

Before she left the office that day, Jenny had been told what her wages would be and that she would be on the same hours and on trial for the month and if good enough, the job would be permanent and her wage would increase. Jenny made her way home on cloud nine. Her mind was full of many thoughts, all of them happy especially when realising she would soon be able to pay some money to her parents to help with the bills and have some left to save for the future, which she could now think more clearly about.

Jenny could hardly contain her happiness when she arrived home and told her parents what had happened that morning. Her dad told her he was so pleased for her, telling her he always knew she was clever and the job would be well suited to her. Betty just grabbed Jenny and hugged her so tightly. Jenny had to ask her to let go stating she could hardly breath, to which Betty apologised stating she was just so happy everything appeared to be coming good for her daughter.

When things calmed down, Betty suggested they should all visit the park and have cake and ice cream to celebrate on the following Saturday, including inviting Jamie to join them. Jenny and her dad thought it was an excellent idea. Jenny mentioned that they should not tell the children until just before going to the park and everyone agreed.

Arriving on time appropriately dressed for the job, Jenny entered Mr Nelson's office and quickly remembered he was not there for the next two weeks. She was just entering the secretary's office adjoining Mr Nelson's when Freda almost bumped into her while coming out of the store room. After greeting Jenny, she showed her which desk would be hers until she retired but explained that Jenny would be spending a lot of time sitting next to her for learning purposes.

The two of them got on very well and Jenny found Freda very patient with her. There weren't many letters to type, though Jenny found out that other employees would give her letters to type as well as Mr Nelsons. Other work consisted of filing and liaising with the warehouse Manager every day to make sure any necessary stock was ordered. Jenny learned quickly and soon got into a good routine. Freda appeared to be pleased with her and at the end of the two weeks, she even told Jenny that she believed Jenny would be an excellent replacement for her.

The work was not hard, but the learning was and Jenny would go home exhausted and with her head full of instructions to do the job. Jenny was well prepared and had made lots of notes which she revisited in the evening when it was quiet. She soon got to grips with everything and even when Mr Nelson returned to the office he treated her very kindly even when mistakes were made, but on the whole it appeared to Jenny that he was happy with her and was sure Freda had given a good report to him.

At the end of the month it was time to say farewell

to Freda. A small gathering was held in the office as she was presented with her retirement gift, a gold watch. It came to Jenny's notice that Freda had been Mr Nelson's secretary for twenty years, so she would be missed a lot. The day after Freda left Mr Nelson told Jenny she was well suited to the job and would therefore be permanent with a pay rise and so Jenny's new work life began.

CHAPTER 26

Saturday arrived and Jenny was looking forward to the trip to the park. During the morning she kept herself busy by writing letters to Renata and the SSAFA sister. She had lots to write about and this time it was all good news. Later, she helped her mum with some household chores until lunch time. After a nice lunch cooked by Jenny and her mum, Amy and Charlie were asked to go and wash their hands and face and put on something nice to wear for a trip out. They weren't told where they were going until they were both ready and then the excitement was clear to see. Jamie arrived and he brought the children a football so they could have a kick about at the park.

At the park, everyone was having fun playing with the ball and riding on the swings and roundabout. Ted suggested that because there were plenty of adults to supervise, he and Jamie should take Amy and Charlie for a boat ride on the lake. It was a rowing boat and the children were even more excited at this prospect.

While the men and children were on the lake, Jenny and her mum were seated on a park bench chatting about this and that. Eventually, Jenny's mum got around to asking Jenny if she had any plans for the future and with a wry smile, she mentioned that she hadn't helped but notice that her friendship with Jamie was looking more serious.

"Oh mum, you are implying that we might be a couple, but I haven't dared to think of Jamie as more than a friend. Besides, he is only trying to be helpful and anyway he is more dad's friend than mine." Jenny felt slightly embarrassed by her mum's enquiries.

"Well, maybe you haven't noticed the way he looks at you and wants to be there for you when problems arrive."

Jenny was thoughtful for a moment, surprised at her mum's suggestions, "You might be right, but I am still married to Roy and with so much that has been happening, I haven't thought of Jamie in a romantic way. I do like him very much though. He is kind and thoughtful and the children seem to like him very much."

"All I am pointing out to you is that he would make a very good catch if you happen to be looking for a new husband."

"That may well be, but I need to be divorced first before I think about a new relationship."

With those last words, they were interrupted by Charlie's shrill voice as he ran up to them after the boat ride, "Mummy did you see me? Did you see me Nanna? I was rowing the boat all by myself. I think I'll be a sailor when I grow up."

Everyone laughed at Charlie's announcement and Jamie, ruffling Charlie's hair, lifted him up high in the air, confirmed that Charlie would make a great sailor. Next on the day's agenda was a visit to the cafe where cake and ice cream was enjoyed by all, so much so that Charlie asked if they could do it all again the next day. In answer to which he was told that this had been a special treat day like the last time they had cake. In answer to Amy's question of what this treat was for, it was explained to her about mummy's new job at her works.

The way home was much quieter and Charlie said he was tired, so Jamie promptly lifted him up onto his shoulders where Charlie fell asleep almost immediately. Jenny smiled and couldn't help thinking that was just like any loving father would do. Maybe her mum was right about him, he would be good husband and father material.

***

The next few weeks were just work and home with nothing in particular happening. Mary paid a visit with Martin and she reported all was going well with the pregnancy. Also, she had letters from both Renata and the SSAFA sister. Both had a surprise for Jenny, Renata was following her husband to Singapore where she would probably live for the next two or so years. While the SSAFA Sister wrote she was so pleased about Jenny's good news and that she too had news of an impending move. She was coming to England to work at the central office where she would remain until her retirement in three years time. She promised that she would take the opportunity to visit Jenny in the future. This pleased Jenny and she couldn't be happier to meet her rescuer again.

Jenny also received two other letters, one from her Solicitor and the other from Roy. The solicitor wrote requesting Jenny to make an appointment to go and visit his office. Roy wrote that he would like to visit her and the children again while he was home visiting his mother. He pointed out that it would only be a day visit to see the children as he was only in England for a weekend. He asked, if possible, the visit could occur the weekend after next, on the Saturday.

She did not inform the children that Roy was coming to visit them and after telling her parents she asked them to not tell the children also.

The Saturday of the visit arrived and after spending an hour in the garden, Roy asked if he could take the children to the park and if she would also come along too. Jenny agreed and Roy was like his old self, very attentive and entertaining towards the children. While Amy and Charlie played on the swings, Jenny and Roy sat on the bench watching them. Roy gave a slight cough and proceeded to speak.

"I have something to tell you. I have been posted to Singapore and will probably be there for at least three years. This will mean I won't be able to visit the children very often, but I will still write letters to them." He waited for Jenny's reaction to this news.

Jenny spoke immediately, "That is good news for you and I hope you are pleased to be visiting another Country, but it will be hard on the children as they always look forward to your visits."

"I am looking forward to going. The whole troop will be going so I will still have my mates with me. I will miss not seeing the children as often and I believe we will be divorced soon so will no longer be able to call you my wife." Roy bowed his head and looked quite sad.

"Yes, my solicitor has asked me to make an appointment, so maybe that is to tell me the divorce will be soon. Have you heard anything from your solicitor?

"No, but I am expecting to very soon. He told me it was almost imminent. It will seem strange being a single man again, but it is all my fault. I lost the love of my life and the chance to be there every day for my children. I must learn to get on with my life and I suppose I will be in the army for many years to come."

Jenny could not say anything to these remarks.

She had been having sad thoughts about their marriage ending but mainly about the children coming to terms with only seeing their daddy whenever he can visit.

Not much was said on the way back to her parents house. Roy was particularly quiet and Jenny could only assume it was because he was feeling sad. After having sandwiches and cake for tea it was time for Roy to leave. He was flying back to Germany early the next morning. There were many hugs and kisses for the children and Roy promised them he would write to them soon, then with a swift goodbye to Jenny he was gone.

The following day Jenny made an appointment with her Solicitor. It was at 2pm the following Thursday.

CHAPTER 27

Jenny went to the Solicitors office straight after work and arrived with time to spare so she did a bit of window shopping to pass the time. Arriving promptly, five minutes early, she knocked on the office door and waited to be asked to enter.

Once inside, a surprise awaited her. Sat behind the large oak desk was a much younger man and Mr Benson was nowhere to be seen.

"Come in Mrs Crabtree and sit down please," pointing to the chair in front of the desk. "I am Mr Carson, standing in for Mr Benson who unfortunately was taken ill and is now in hospital. Do not worry though I am up to speed with your divorce case."

"Oh, I hope he is alright and it is not too serious. I like Mr Benson very much and he was very kind and explained everything thoroughly to me."

"Well I hope you will like me too. However this will perhaps be the only time you have to visit me because I have arranged this visit to tell you that the court has dealt with your divorce and it went in your favour. In six weeks time when the Decree Nisi comes through, you will officially be a single woman again and your marriage to Mr Roy Crabtree will be at an end."

Jenny gave a little gasp covering her mouth with her hand. "I can hardly believe this has happened at last. I seem to have been waiting forever for this divorce to happen."

"Believe me, it has happened and you have sole custody of Amy and Charlie Crabtree with visiting rights to be arranged by yourself and Mr Crabtree. He will also be making a monthly payment to you for these two children, but unfortunately you have not been granted any money for yourself due to the fact that you left him and so ended the marriage."

His voice appeared to reverberate around the room and Jenny sat silent unable to find any words to what had just been told to her by Mr Carson. Her thoughts dashed around haphazardly in her mind. After a moment of silence had passed, she found her voice once again and as a single tear rolled down her cheek she managed to let him know that she understood all that he had told her and was very grateful for all the help she had received.

"I do hope the tears are happy ones on hearing this news. I understand it can also be a sad time because you have many memories of being married to Mr Crabtree." He hesitated for a moment then spoke again more hurriedly, "Of course, under the circumstances of why you left your husband, some of your memories would not be happy ones perhaps"

"My tears are for my happiness and relief that it is finally over and I can now plan my future and put the past behind me."

"Well, then it only remains for me to hand over the official court papers and let you know that the Decree Nisi will be posted to you when it comes through to me. May I wish you all good luck for the future and there is nothing more to say but wish you happiness from now on."

Jenny shook his hand and asked him to pass on a message to Mr Benson, thanking him for his work and wishing him a speedy recovery. With that she left the office and slowly walked to the bus stop to travel home, at the same time wondering how she was going to tell the children that they will not live with their daddy any more. She knew, at least they thought Roy was a loving father and that they in turn loved him.

Once home, her parents were delighted for her that she was finally divorced from the man they felt nothing but anger and hatred. Her mum though, could sense that Jenny was feeling all manner of emotions and so she wrapped an arm around her daughter and with the other hand, gently stroked her hair. Jenny just let the tears fall with soft sobs while remaining silent. Finally she was able to speak again and told her parents that she was sad that her marriage to Roy had been filled with horrible memories of violence and unhappiness. She told them that when trying to remember happy times in her marriage it was very difficult to think of any but there must have been some, like the births of Amy and Charlie, but they were spoiled by thoughts of the times she endured abuse from Roy. She continued by saying that she could wish she had never married Roy but then she would not have the children and she couldn't regret having them.

When she had finished speaking, her dad tried to

ease his daughter's pain by telling her that she should forget the past and start a new life. Stating that she could have many happy times ahead of her if she just allows herself to create future happy memories.

Later that day, Jamie came to visit and he sat quietly listening to Jenny pouring out all her troubles of the past few years. When at last she had finished, he gave her a cuddle telling her that whatever she had planned for her future, their friendship would always remain and he would be there for her always. This pleased her a lot and a strange feeling of love came over her for this kind man who had demanded nothing but friendship from her and she felt safe and warm wrapped in his arms. Betty smiled as she looked on at them and she gave a soft sigh.

When it was time to tell the children, Jenny was nervous to see their reaction to the news of her divorce from their daddy. She needn't have worried because Charlie just remarked "poor daddy, he will be sad he can't live with us" then went off to play in the garden. Amy, however, had the reaction Jenny had feared. She burst into tears not saying anything and all Jenny could do was to cuddle her until the sobbing ceased.

Afterwards, being ever the inquisitive girl she

was, there were many questions Jenny had to answer until at last Amy was satisfied that she had all the details of what their future would be like. Still feeling a bit sad, she went off to her room to write a letter for her daddy. The next morning, all signs of tears or sadness had gone. Jenny, instead, put on a happy face and a relaxed attitude, determined to start the future in a more positive way and help her children come to terms with the divorce and the new life ahead.

CHAPTER 28

Six months after the divorce, Amy and Charlie had gone up a year and into a new class at school and Jenny was well established in her role as secretary at work. Mary had a baby girl, who was named Sophie, and both mother and baby were doing well.

Jenny had found herself getting closer to Jamie and now they were in a romantic relationship. Her parents were so happy that Jamie and Jenny were getting on so well. Betty had stated that she always knew Jamie had feelings for her daughter and secretly had wanted them to be a couple. Recently, Jenny and the children had started staying weekends at Jamie's house where he cooked meals for them and the children were so excited and liked his home very much. Jenny was pleased that the children felt so comfortable at Jamie's house as the intention was for them to spend many more weekends there.

Roy had still not visited the children yet, but had promised he would definitely try to get to England to visit in another month. He had kept his promise and wrote letters often and in one had asked Amy to tell her mummy that he wasn't alone any more but had met a nice young woman.

Another letter arrived for Jenny and in it Roy explained about his new girlfriend. She was the sister of his best mate in the army so they had become friends. He had met her many times whilst visiting his mates home and they had become close and been on several dates before he left for Singapore. He stated that they had stayed in contact over the months he had been away and he liked her very much and hoped she would come with him to meet his children when he visited, if that was alright with Jenny. There weren't any objections from Jenny, she was pleased he had a girlfriend but found it strange that they had a long distance relationship.

Jenny wrote back to Roy, enclosing yet more drawings from Amy and Charlie. Informing Roy that everyone was looking forward to his visit with his girlfriend, Catherine, and asking him to let her know of the date when they would be coming.

When Jenny told Jamie about Roy having a girlfriend, he seemed more than happy to hear this news. Later it would be revealed why he was so happy as when on a date with Jenny at a restaurant, Jamie got down on one knee and with a ring, he asked Jenny to marry him. Jenny was slightly shocked by his actions but immediately and without any doubts, accepted his offer of marriage.

Everyone was so happy to hear the news of their engagement. Telling them all that the wedding would be a Christmas one and they would have a big party to celebrate. Amy was so excited and immediately asked if she would be a bridesmaid and was told the answer was a definite yes and that Charlie would be a page boy.

A further surprise came in a letter from Tom, her brother, who had also got engaged and was now back in an army camp in England. His Fiance was called Mandy and they would be pleased to come to Jenny's wedding. So, not only would the family all be at her wedding, but they would be having a family Christmas too. Jenny couldn't have been any happier. Hopefully she will never hear sorry from now on.

If you enjoyed this book, then why not try other titles by the same author…

Doctor in Disguise
by Christine Diggins

1960s Lancashire and Kate Andrews, a nurse and mother of two young boys struggles with a difficult job as she also deals with the twists and turns of working on a busy surgical ward at St Mark's Hospital. Things take a turn when a new junior doctor arrives on the ward bringing a secret past that unbeknown to Kate she was a part of.

Romance and conflict ensue as the mystery slowly unravels with Kate having to keep a cloak of secrecy from those who would ruin her career.

Will Kate overcome the challenges of keeping the secret while maintaining the professionalism expected of her?

A Seven Day Wonder

by Christine Diggins

1946 and Sally Ann is born into the family of Charlie and Lizzie Booth. They have four other children and the family live in Lancashire. At the age of nineteen, Sally is preparing to leave home and as she packs her suitcase, she reflects on the various memories she has from the age of twelve after moving into this home on Greenbank Estate. This is Sally Ann's story from that first day until she must now leave it all behind her. The memories of growing up are of happy and some scary times. Always with one ambition mapping her future she reminisces of how her life revolved around family, friends, and events. The worst of these would be burned into her memory forever. Has she the confidence and is she strong enough to start a new chapter of her life? With help from her family and her special friend, the farmers son, she just might succeed.